FROM AFAR FOREVER

by NICOLÁS MIHOVILOVIĆ
Translated by Elisabeth Jezierski

Note from Mirta Mihovilović
For additional information about this work visit
www.fromafarforever.com

Copyright © 2007 by Mirta Mihovilović and
Elisabeth Jezierski
First edition: January 2009
Second edition July 2011

ISBN: 978-0-615-25612-2
Publisher Mirta Mihovilović, Chapel Hill, NC
Printed in US by InstantPublisher.com
Library of Congress Control Number: 2008909303

Cover Design: Mary Dimercurio Prasad
Cover photo: © (1995) Mirta Mihovilović,
Parque Nacional Torres del Paine

Contents

About the Author

Born in Punta Arenas, Chile in 1916 to a family of Croatian émigrés, Nicolás Mihovilović Rajčević, the oldest of three brothers, was the first proficient Spanish speaker in his family. He completed high school at the Liceo Fiscal de Hombres de Punta Arenas where, in his senior year, he was editor of the school magazine "Germinal". An avid reader, he participated in local literary festivals since his youth; he was interested in politics and, from 1946 to 1950, he was Governor of Tierra del Fuego. In 1953 he moved to Santiago, maintaining close contacts with literary circles of the capital. He explored the art of cinematography and, in the late fifties, taught history of the cinema at the Universidad Católica de Santiago. In 1966 he published his first novel, *Desde Lejos Para Siempre* (*From Afar Forever*), followed, in 1974, by *Entre el Cielo y el Silencio* (*Only Sky and Solitude*) and in 1978 by *En El Ultimo Mar del Mundo* (*The Remotest Sea in the World*). These three novels form a trilogy depicting the lives of city dwellers, country folks and seamen in Southern Chile and Argentina during the early XX century. These novels were followed by *Estampas Magallánicas / Cuatro Hombres de Ayer y Siempre* (*Images from Magallanes / Four Men to Remember from Yesteryear*) and Simbad Sin Mar / *Semi-cuentos* (*Quasi-stories*) in 1984. Shortly before his death in Quilpue, in 1986, he was elected a member of the Academia Chilena de la Lengua. His work is still poignant and in print. *Desde Lejos Para Siempre* is in its 6th Spanish edition, *En el Último Mar del Mundo, Estampas Magallánicas* and *Semi-Cuentos* all are in their 2nd edition. Two of his works, *Desde Lejos Para Siempre*, and his *Semi-Cuentos* (*Iz Daleka Zauvijek* and *Ludi Keko*) were published in Croatian in 2003 and 2005, respectively. *From Afar Forever* is the first of his works to be translated into English.

Works by the Author

Desde Lejos Para Siempre. 1966 (Eros, Santiago, Chile). 1985 (La Noria, Santiago, Chile), 1996, 1997, 1999, 2007 (Ediciones Dálmatas, Punta Arenas, Chile).

Entre el Cielo y el Silencio. 1974 (Pineda Libros, Santiago, Chile).

En el Último Mar del Mundo. 1978 (Zig-Zag, Santiago Chile), 1997 (Ediciones Dálmatas, Punta Arenas, Chile). Premio Municipalidad de Santiago (1979).

Estampas Magallánicas / Cuatro Hombres de Ayer y Siempre. 1984 (La Noria, Santiago, Chile), 2007 (Ediciones Dálmatas, Punta Arenas, Chile).

Simbad Sin Mar / Semi-Cuentos. 1984 (Sociedad de Escritores de Valparaíso), 1987 (Edición de Homenaje).

Croatian Translations

Iz Daleka Zauvijek. 2003 (Naklada Bošković, Split, Croatia).

Ludi Keko. 2005 (Naklada Bošković, Split, Croatia).

English Translations

From Afar Forever. 2009 (Chile and Dalmatia Publishing House, Chapel Hill, North Carolina.

About the Translator

Born in Vienna, Austria in 1924, Elisabeth Jezierski had a multilingual upbringing. She spent her childhood in Austria and Germany and moved with her family to Argentina in 1938. She came to the United States in 1947 and since 1958 has made her home in Durham, North Carolina. In 1949 she graduated from Bryn Mawr with a Bachelor's Degree (*magna cum laude*) in Politics and Russian history. In 1952 she earned a Master's Degree in Slavic Literatures and Languages at Harvard and from 1965 to 1969 was enrolled in the Doctoral Program in Romance Languages at the University of North Carolina at Chapel Hill.

She was a member of the International Studies Group of the Brookings Institution from 1949 to 1951. She began her long and on-going career in tutoring as a teenager in Buenos Aires. She was a tutor for the Harvard Bureau of Study Counsel from 1954 to 1958, an interpreter for the American Dance Festival, the Sister Cities Program and the North Carolina International Visitors' Center. From 1952 to 1989 she held appointments at the Cambridge School of Weston, Duke University, North Carolina Central and North Carolina State University, teaching French, German, Spanish, Russian, and Russian literature in English translation. She taught English at the Pedagogical Institute of Durham's Sister City Kostroma in Russia. She was the recipient of two grants from the International Research and Exchanges Board at Moscow State University in 1975 and 1980, two grants from the National Endowment for the Humanities at the Ohio State University in 1976 and the University of Minnesota in 1983, a Fulbright grant at the University of Rome in 1981 and an award from the Folger Institute at the Library of Congress in 1986.

She has been involved in many editorial and translation projects. Her translation of the short story "Going after Goat Antelopes" by Svetlana Vasilenko, appears in *Lives in Transit: A Collection of Recent Russian Women's writing*, edited by Helena Goscilo (Ardis, Dana Point, CA, 1995). She was the consultant for the visual translation of *Mayakovsky / El Lissitsky: For the Voice* by Martha Scotford (The British Library, 2000) and the translator of numerous passages quoted in the monograph *Nikolai Karamzin: from Nature to History - An Interpretation* by Vladimir Bilenkin to be published by the Edwin Mellen Press. The Appendix to this work contains the first English translation of Karamzin's fictional correspondence between the friends Melodor and Fialet—a seminal work of 18th century Russian literature and thought.

Foreword

It is a great pleasure for me to introduce to the English-speaking reader this work that is so close to my heart. More than forty years ago my father gave me a copy of the first edition of *Desde Lejos Para Siempre (From Afar Forever)*. It was the best birthday present I have ever received. Reading the novel brought into my life the life of my grandparents and others of their generation, who came to Punta Arenas, Chile, and, braving a myriad of uncertainties, found their "norte" in the southernmost region of the Americas.

At the beginning of the twentieth century, the port of Punta Arenas, an obligatory stop for every ship sailing between the Pacific and Atlantic Oceans, received an influx of European emigrants. Along with the native Chileans, they energized the region: men and women, overcoming the vicissitudes of the past, living in the present and resolutely looking toward the future. These are the characters of *From Afar Forever*. Their intertwined stories unfold between 1920 and 1940 and provide a firsthand account of this southern city. For these reasons *From Afar Forever* has become part of the patrimony of the Magellan region.

According to my father, he was in first grade when, confronted by lessons taught in Spanish, he recognized the need to belong, to be accepted outside the family circle. Thus, Spanish became his dominant language, while Dalmatian, the Croatian dialect spoken by his elders, remained his way to communicate at home. In reconciling these two modes of expression, my father found his voice. Throughout his youth, while studying and working, he wrote poems and short stories. Four decades after that first school year, he decided to revise a handful of his stories and give fluidity to their narrative: the novel *From Afar Forever* was born.

This English edition was preceded by the recent appearance of *From Afar Forever* in Croatian (Editorial Bosković, Split 2003) almost half a century after its first Spanish-language edition in 1966. This has been possible because over the years there were people who, moved by the account, felt the need to preserve it both in my native Chile (five Spanish editions between 1966 and 2000) and in Croatia.

Now it is Elisabeth Jezierski who transmits my father's voice through her translation. My thanks go to her and to Christi Stanforth for her editorial expertise.

I also take this opportunity to thank Jerko Ljubetić, Adnan Nogo, Ines Batinić-Haberle, and Sandra Savić for their help with Croatian; Philip Jezierski for his input on colloquialisms; Domingo Mihovilović (Tessier),

Nedjieljka Pavlov, Zdenka Martinović, Myrna López, Griselda Mihovilović and Margarita Mihovilović Perić, the crew from Punta Arenas that always had the right answer; and Odesa Pavlov, Yvelise Alvarado and Tomás Čekalović, important conduits of information. My thanks also go to Mary Prasad for sharing her knowledge of boccie ball and cover design; to Richard Berkley for his help with maritime terminology; to Nora Segilman Favorov and Mirtha Umaña-Murray for their utmost generosity with their time and editing abilities; to Lawrence Lazarus, who one evening in the mid-1980s told me that I should see this book translated into English; to Alberto Politoff and Carmen Lucaveche, who were part of this project from the outset; and to Patricia Marticorena for her steadfast support, which will allow her to see this project completed.

I believe that the English translation will resonate no less with the multiethnic readers of North America, for the great majority of them are also immigrants or descendants of immigrants.

To quote my father in Spanish tinged with a Chilean inflection: ¡A leer se ha dicho! (Time to start reading!)

Mirta Mihovilović Pavlov

Chapel Hill, North Carolina

March 19, 2007

---

xi

FROM AFAR FOREVER

by NICOLÁS MIHOVILOVIĆ

To my daughter Mirta,
in remembrance of those who,
having come from afar like her grandparents,
looked at the sea with nostalgia,
yet remained—in us—
in our land
forever.

1

TÍO JUAN

I don't exactly remember the year or the month, but I do remember it was a Saturday. The fierce Magellanic wind had sprung up early on, almost at daybreak. It must have been about five in the morning when Mama took the fragrant golden loaves of bread out of the old Dover stove. Things were not as she would have liked them to be, but still, she seemed content. The wind roared across the roof and pulled at the stove's flames, which rushed up the stovepipe, hissing like a blowtorch. The black tin stovepipe——polished every week with a special wax—turned red-hot.

My father's heavy footsteps made the floor creak as he waited for his shaving water to boil. He had penetrating gray eyes and an impressive brown handlebar moustache. He kept humming a popular little waltz, the inevitable Tuscan cigar[1] between his lips. From our vantage point, he seemed gigantic.

With a finality that showed he had been thinking about this problem for a long time, Papa said, "It won't last beyond this summer. All the boards will have to be replaced. I could go through the floor at any moment."

Above the howling of the wind you could hear the rain starting to slam against the planks of the walls and the roof. The stove spewed out puffs of coal smoke. Mama remarked, "All the fire's going up the stovepipe! If this storm doesn't let up, I won't be able to roast the chicken." Then, without missing a beat, she shouted at the youngest boy, "Zvonko, stop that! No snitching hot bread! You'll get a bellyache!"

The boy trotted off contritely and went to press his forehead against the cold windowpane, but the unbridled fury of the rain and the wind pounding against the glass frightened him. Shuffling his feet, he climbed onto the woodbox next to the stove.

There Mama handed him a mug filled to the brim with hot milk, mixed with a dash of brewed coffee, and a thick slice of the bread, by now sufficiently cool. The three-year-old sucked up his snot and smiled; he dipped the bread into the steaming mug and, before Mama could prevent it, had made a big mess. She patiently took away

---

[1] A Tuscan cigar was thick in the middle and tapered at both ends. It was customary to cut it in half to make two cigars out of one.

his mug, made him blow his nose into her immaculate handkerchief, tied a bib of imposing dimensions around his neck, and let him have his fun with breakfast. We, the four older ones, at our designated places around the table, watched, somewhat enviously, how our little brother stuck his hand into his mug, oblivious of the "teaspoon rule," and was allowed to slouch rather than sit upright like a fence post on one of our wooden chairs, which was made—like all the chairs in the house—to withstand our father's 120 kilos.

At six Papa went to open the door of our corner *boliche*.[2] Precise like a stopwatch, the first customer of the day was Oyarzún, a native of Chiloé Island,[3] a dark-skinned, stocky cart driver with a droopy black moustache. He never failed to stop by early each morning to buy a pack of cheap cigarettes before settling down at the counter to have a brandy prepared "the Austrian way."

The exchange with Oyarzún was my father's first conversation each day and, unquestionably, as important to him as our daily bread. The conversation was comfortable: Papa did all the talking, and Oyarzún

---

[2] Small general store, usually located on a street corner.

[3] Main island of the archipelago by the same name, located off the coast of Chile, 1,300 kilometers to the north of Punta Arenas. Due to the prosperity of Punta Arenas—a required stop for all ships traveling between the Pacific and the Atlantic Oceans prior to the construction of the Panama Canal—natives of the Chiloé archipelago migrated South and settled in Punta Arenas and adjacent areas.

listened with exaggerated attention, knowing full well that after the first glass, the "Austrian"[4] would pour him half a glass free of charge. Once Oyarzún had again taken his place in front of his oxen, and the cart, overloaded with large pieces of split lumber, had moved off, swaying along the wide, deserted street, Papa would have a quick drink and return to our kitchen.

The four of us older boys were ready to go out: we had our canvas bags, and our shoes were shined. Here and there, a new patch graced our pants. Papa gave us the once-over: nails, hair, gloves, caps, buttons...

That stormy morning, as on so many other occasions, we walked along hanging from my father's arms in a cluster, clinging to him as to something indestructible, something considerably more powerful than the fury of the eighty-kilometer-per-hour wind that was trying to drag us to the very sea.

From the hillside where our house stood, it was the sea that greeted us as we came through the door; we always stopped briefly to look at it. That morning the bay was boiling with foam. The smaller boats were dancing a furious jig, moored to their buoys, and the larger ships— one English, one Greek, two German, and a Navy

---

[4] In Chile's Magellanic region South Slavic immigrants—mostly Croats, who had come to the area at the time their homeland was under the rule of the Austro-Hungarian Empire—were often referred to as "Austrian," a name with a more or less pejorative connotation.

revenue cutter—were riding out the storm at a distance, almost lost in a mist of seawater raised by the hurricane.

That Saturday the sea acquired a special meaning. For about a month now we had known that this was the day Tío Juan—Barba[5] Ive as we heard him called at home—was to arrive from Europe. But unless the storm subsided, no ship would be able to enter the port. Papa scowled, the tips of his moustache disheveled by the wind and soaked with rain. He muttered a curse; then, as if to soften his words and turn the whole thing into a joke, he added two slightly more innocuous expressions, one Croatian and one Spanish: "*Bogami. Mierda.*"[6]

The school was almost deserted. (Not many people believed you absolutely could not skip class unless you were sick). Señorita Julia, our teacher, had brought her harp. That morning she taught us singing until eleven; then, seeing that the weather was not improving, she let us go half an hour early. One by one, she helped us into our overcoats, put on our caps and gloves, and saw to it that our satchels were secure; she told the older children to take care of the younger ones, made us cross ourselves, and held the door half open so we could leave.

---

[5] "Uncle" in Croatian.
[6] "My God. Shit!"

Tossed about by the wind, splashing through puddles, bent low so the blinding cold rain wouldn't sting our eyes, we struggled up the steep grade. Our house was barely four blocks away; nonetheless, a moment came when we simply couldn't go any farther: the onslaught of the rain was choking us. We turned our backs to the wind until we had caught our breath; then we tried to continue uphill, sliding in the mud. Alexander, the youngest in the group, stopped dead and, clutching at a picket fence, started to cry. My other two brothers followed suit. Never had I felt so helpless. It was terrible! The four of us huddled together like four abandoned chicks. For the first time in my life I understood that even children could die. The rain had drenched us. With our arms thrown around each other, shaking not so much from the cold as from fear, all four of us were crying. Suddenly the wind ripped off my cap. I tried to run after it, slipped, and fell in the mud.

Almost at once I felt myself being lifted up by a powerful grip. It was Oyarzún. I smiled at him despite my tears, despite the mud that covered me. He said, "All right, 'little Austrian,' lend me a hand with your brothers." One by one, he lifted us onto the now empty cart, on its way back to the hills, straining against the savage storm.

Oyarzún's poncho was dripping with water, his moustache droopier than ever; there was no way he could light his cigarette. Crouched next to us on the rickety floor of the cart, he called to his oxen, "All right, Clavel, all right, Pampa. Today we'se goin' to get us a free drink... What did they send them kids to school for?"

Mama virtually tore us out of Oyarzún's arms and, in less than two minutes, had us all in bed, clay hot water bottles at our feet. With the ease that lets children leap straight from anxiety to the greatest happiness, we were very soon in an uproar, jumping from bed to bed. But Papa saw fit to look in on us and one glance of his reduced us to the most profound silence. It seemed best to remain quiet, at least for a while. Through the thin partition we could hear the voice of the cart driver, rasping and unhurried as always: "Good thing them kids go to school, so they won't have to get screwed like the likes of me; but af'er all, when God makes a day fit for dogs, it's more better for Christians to stay home. You should've seen how hard your oldest tried to pull his little brothers uphill. He's got guts, that guy, he's got guts. But the smallest one, oh, my! He was actually dragging his satchel on the ground. Here's to you!"

A long silence followed. Then we heard two glasses clink. We knew that my father, at a loss for words, was choking back a tear.

At three o'clock the storm suddenly died down and the sun came out. My father, relieved, said sententiously, "There isn't a Saturday without sunshine." And then he added, pointing to Alexander and me, "You two are coming with me." He said this affectionately, as if he were awarding us a prize, or giving us a present.

***

Leaving us off at the kiosk of the "Green Pier"—an obligatory destination for the inhabitants of Punta Arenas after Sunday mass and a place of great commotion every time a ship arrived—Papa, with the agility of an old sailor, jumped into the launch taking off to meet the steamer that had just come in and was anchored half a mile offshore. The hoarse hooting of the boat, and handkerchiefs waved in the distance, prompted the waving of handkerchiefs on the dock. There were some elegant ladies in high boots with white buttons, wearing wide-brimmed hats decorated with flowers. An old skinny cop nicknamed "Three Piers," three red stars on his sleeves and an enormous saber knocking against his calves, strutted back and forth as if he owned the whole jetty; a little white dog followed him everywhere.

Our eyes were on Papa, who, scorning the seats on the launch, remained standing, ramrod-straight and wide-legged on the small deck at the bow, holding onto his hat with his right hand and twisting his moustache with his left. The boat was pitching and rocking in seas still churning from the recent storm. We thought our father was heroic to sail in such a small craft, and we found it amazing that he stood as erect in the pitching boat as he did on solid ground.

The launch disappeared from view behind the ship flying the Italian flag. Old "Three Piers" by now felt that he owned the entire bay and started explaining to all who cared to listen that because the sea was still very rough, the launch was being brought alongside on the lee of the steamer, where it would be better sheltered.

***

Tío Juan limped slightly; he was tall and slender. His eyes were blue, his hair blond, and he had a sad smile. He sported a tiny trim moustache that seemed comical to us. He did not wear a tie. His jacket was too short and his pants too tight. His yellow shoes creaked at every step, one shoe more than the other. He carried a black suitcase and a coffee-colored canvas bag, doubtlessly too big for its contents.

Once more we hung onto Papa like a cluster of grapes and left the pier. Our uncle followed behind, struggling with his luggage and his limp. We boys had to run to keep up with our father's large strides. Papa stopped at the square at the end of the pier, next to the small tower and its clock—which marked the hours, days, and lunar phases—and looked around. We saw a string of carriages, their tops up, hitched to droopy-eared horses, attended by anxious cabbies waiting for passengers. We climbed into the carriage that was fifth in line. The coachman was Papa's cousin. We called him Barba Jule.

After Tío Juan had been introduced and polite greetings exchanged, we listened all the long way home to a novel type of conversation, made up of memories and events from a far-off world, a world that was strange and yet ours. Tío Juan admired my sturdy shoes, impervious to water and snow, and compared them to the cheap, lightweight footwear "back there," the *opanke*[7] made from untanned goat hide. Mama had often mentioned them.

I eyed the suitcase and the canvas bag the long-awaited Tío Juan had brought to America and mused that more than one surprise might emerge from there. Uncles who visited our house always brought something for their nephews. Given that this one had come from a place so far away, I wondered, how much more might he have brought?

That night our gathering didn't break up until late. Even Barba Jule stayed on after the grilled chicken and the delicious applestrudel to savor a glass of the *prošek*[8] Tío Juan had brought from his native land.

By that time I was already in bed under a mountain of blankets, trying not to fall asleep so I could keep listening to the lively conversation. It was very late when I heard my father get up from the table to light the

---

[7] Peasant shoes without heels, often with a pointed tip, the top woven of leather strips, covering the foot completely.

[8] Sweet aged wine.

paraffin streetlamp; finally he bolted the door. I fell asleep at dawn.

On Sunday morning, when we were getting ready to have breakfast—coffee with hot milk and fresh bread with clotted cream—we heard Tío Juan's halting steps; he appeared, carrying a little parcel, which he put in the center of the table, saying, *"Dobro jutro.* Good Morning." Mama undid the white cloth wrapping and took from it a small, pungent goat cheese, which she kissed, strangely moved, just as she kissed her bread when it came out of the oven. Turning to my father, she asked him to divide the cheese among us. At that time I didn't understand all the fuss about some cheese I didn't even like because it made my tongue burn.

After that Tío Juan pulled out of his odd jacket a package of almond candy and gave us each a piece. The candy was delicious, but it seemed our uncle had a sweet tooth himself, because he didn't give us any more.

We went to eight o'clock mass with Mama (we'd got up too late to make it to the earlier one), and by half past nine we were back, ready to help with the chores. Papa and Tío Juan went out, and we didn't see them again until noon, when they came home to have lunch.

Mama had prepared gnocchis and an excellent roast. Even little Zvonko had been pulled up to the table in his high chair. Protected by his huge bib, he sucked at his piece of meat with relish until he had reduced it to shreds. These he threw on the floor, totally indifferent to the hard work the rest of us had endured to make it shine.

Tío Juan spoke nervously and asked many questions. He was concerned about quickly finding a good job so he could save some money and return home. Evidently he thought Punta Arenas wasn't a town where he'd like to stay for good. People spoke an incomprehensible language and lived in absurd houses built out of tin, lined on the inside with thin sheets of wood. By contrast, "over there" everything was built of solid stone. Here there were neither fig trees nor grapevines, neither olive trees nor flowers. You had to walk in the mud, along streets full of potholes and puddles; drunkards, and ugly dirty people everywhere.

My mother kept a discreet silence. Maybe she agreed with her brother. My father coughed to clear his throat, which was irritated from all his smoking, and said, "We all came here thinking the streets were lined with gold, that all you had to do was to fill a sack and return to our Dalmatia, to our village and to our wonderful climate. But then, one day, we see ourselves surrounded by children, by friends who once were strangers. We look at the sea, which is always present, ready for us to take off whenever we feel like it, and suddenly we're in no hurry to go back. Over there you have the same old people, the same eternal stones, without the slightest change, just as we left them. Here, on the other hand, you see something new every day, because this is a new land and every day we marvel a bit at this newness. You work hard, but you've got something to show for it. You build a little house; when it begins to feel cramped, you enlarge it. You put some lettuce seeds in the ground; no sooner do the seedlings come up than the wind destroys them for you; so you remind yourself you're a man and keep on sowing, one, two, even three times. In the end, one day you'll be eating lettuce and realize you're tasting victory. Back home you'll keep on singing the same songs, hearing the same voices, looking at the same clouds. Yes, all of that is beautiful, but we left it behind, because we felt the scenery and the atmosphere and, above all, existence itself to be confining. Back home you can enjoy life; here you actually live it. I'm saying all this, because that's what I truly believe."

If Mama and Tío Juan thought differently, they kept it to themselves. Mama looked at her brother questioningly, but he either couldn't find an answer or didn't care to say what was on his mind.

My father, to relieve the tension, offered him a cigar, and soon the whole house was filled with tobacco smoke.

***

Tío Juan spent the entire week visiting or receiving visits from relatives and compatriots, which at times cheered him up and at times made him sad. Occasionally I had to accompany him so he wouldn't get lost in the unfamiliar streets. He walked in silence, slowly, so his slight limp wouldn't be noticeable, looking about as though he were waiting to glimpse something worth seeing. And so another Sunday rolled around.

Toward nine o'clock that morning Papa, impeccable in his black suit, his watch chain draped across his belly, his tie held by the clip studded with a gold nugget, filled two small glasses with *rakija*[9] and invited Tío Juan to have some salted sardines and hot bread. After the men had a second drink, we all went out to the square.

A lot was going on there. The central kiosk (a sort of gazebo with windowpanes, topped by a flat cupola shaped like a meringue) had been moved to one side. Now it covered up one of the four fountains that marked each of the four cardinal directions, and there the Magellan Battalion Band was playing, making more noise than music.

The center of the square was now to be the site of a monument to the Portuguese explorer Ferdinand Magellan, who four centuries ago sailed the strait that now bears his name to unite the Atlantic and the Pacific Oceans. He reached the Philippines, where he died in a

---

[9] A type of brandy made from grapes (also called *grappa*).

rain of arrows, making it possible for a Spanish ship to claim the glory of circumnavigating the globe for the first time. It was he who had baptized the region Tierra del Fuego in honor of the bonfires lit by the Ona Indians along part of his daring southern route; it was likewise Magellan who had named Patagonia[10] for the unusually large prints left in the snow by the guanaco-hide footgear of the Tehuelches.[11]

Rumor had it that the monument would be extremely tall and that the first strong gust of wind might topple it. In any case, the hole dug for the base was considerable—wide and deep enough to hold a whole house. A compact fence of thick planks had been put up to prevent anyone from falling into that huge pit. My father explained to Tío Juan what was going on, but evidently our uncle was thinking of other, faraway matters.

The clock struck ten. From the steeple came the cold chime of bells—brief, penetrating sounds—followed, at the end of a discordant peal, by three bronze strokes announcing High Mass.

For me this mass was like a party. The warm, well-lit church seemed like a different place from the cold, dark church of the seven o'clock mass to which our

---

[10] Land of the large feet.
[11] Land dwellers of Patagonia, a region of southern Chile and southern Argentina.

mother usually took us. Tirelessly recited rosaries and the throng of old women receiving communion dragged out that early service for what seemed an eternity; to make matters worse, there always were several somber-looking priests, stiffly emerging from the cubicles of the confessionals.

High Mass, on the other hand, began with music; you could hear the hum of voices. The male members of the congregation entered with energetic steps, many of them staying in the back of the nave, near the portals, surreptitiously looking at the women. Here was Don Pedro, the baker; Uncle Jozo, Kum[12] Jakov, and another dozen and a half of our friends and relatives. They all affected carefully combed moustaches, carried themselves rigidly like poles, necks unbending, and wore their inevitable black Sunday suits with flamboyant ties; the most daring ones wore shoes of colored leather. All of them—as if to celebrate their Dalmatian origin—sported flowers in their buttonholes, and most of them held their hats at chest level. I amused myself by comparing these hats. There were broad-brimmed hats, hats with wide or narrow bands, hats with flat or high crowns, hats made of felt or velvet, even a few bowlers. The most distinguished among them was the brilliant pearl gray hat of the elegant Barba Marko Radojković. Among that Sunday's crowd I

---

[12] Close friend, best man, or godfather (in this case the latter).

noticed two officers with their long buttoned-up frock coats, tightly fitting black pants, and boots pointed like knives. There were people of all social classes whom I did not know, but I did recognize the children of the rich Spaniards of our town. My whole life I'd been hearing talk about the Menéndez, Campos, and Montes families and several others I got mixed up, because I had also heard Swiss, French, English, and German surnames: apparently they were all well-to-do burghers. By contrast, we "Austrians" and Italians were poor, although a few of us were beginning to put on airs of prosperity. Those successful ones no longer attended mass. Instead they strolled around the square just like the Protestants, the two or three "Turkish"[13] vendors of fabric trims and lengths of cashmere, and an occasional Jew who, having spent his Saturday praying, now had to spend his Sunday walking about to no purpose, enviously examining and reexamining the handsome mansions that surrounded the square.

The sound of the organ and my curiosity made mass go by quickly. I was especially amused by the hat of a lady sitting quite far in front, in one of the first rows. A lady could never, for any reason, sit among the men, just as it was forbidden for the men to sit on the right side of the nave, reserved for the women. That's why the

---

[13] These "Turks" actually came from various Arab countries and had emigrated to avoid being subjects of the Ottoman Empire.

bachelors preferred to hang out in back, where the demarcation line was blurred in a free zone of benches and prie-dieus. The hat that had caught my eye was purple and had little veils, lace, flowers, and other trimmings I couldn't make out exactly. It occupied the space of three persons, and its owner—or, rather, the lady owned by the hat—couldn't move her head a fraction of a centimeter for fear of knocking against the hairdos of her neighbors, covered by black mantillas. It was quite obviously an irreverent hat, and to it were riveted fifty pairs of eyes belonging to the males crowding around the church doors in the rear.

The final chords of the organ roared thunderously. Thanks to the efforts of the sexton, the great central portal opened wide as if by a miracle, and the worshippers slowly made their exit. The dandies from the back unhurriedly filed out to the vestibule and, taking up positions on both sides, allowed the rest of the congregation to pass. My father, my uncle, and I walked right through the center and stopped on the sidewalk, next to the people who had finished their stroll around the square. The large hat approached, undulating above the heads of the crowd. Tío Juan stood on tiptoe in his yellow boots while my father twisted his moustache, looking down calmly from his height.

The lady passed by us. My father took off his hat and bowed slightly. The lady returned his greeting with a nod and a trace of a smile. Fifty angry pairs of eyes glared at my father. Many bit their moustaches, disgusted.

Once back home, my father talked about the incident, laughing merrily: "They looked like fools, and when I told them I'd had this woman sitting on my knees, they almost went berserk." But it was true. Fifteen years back, when this elegant lady—the one who now turned the heads of all the bachelors in town—was a little girl, she had indeed sat on my Papa's lap. At the time, he was paving the courtyard at the French Consulate. The little girl was the consul's daughter. This was the first time I saw my Tío Juan laugh so hard that tears came to his eyes.

Occasionally Papa said something conceited and disconcerting; but he knew that if the courtyard needed repaving, he'd be the one to be called.

We had a cheerful lunch. Even Mama was joking and talking animatedly, telling her brother amusing episodes and reminiscing about their childhood. We listened intently. We barely understood any of it, but one thing was certain: this was a beautiful day in every way. Outside the sun was shining. The chickens were having a great time, pecking about for worms. The dog dozed next to his doghouse. You could hear the sound of a scratchy phonograph from next door.

Around two o'clock that afternoon, Tía Keka arrived with her five lads. The oldest was already in long pants, but the others, like us, wore sailor suits, our Sunday best. There were enough sailors to man a warship, though our cousins' suits were navy blue, and ours gray; to be sure our collars and cuffs had three stripes, while theirs had only two.

The sun had dried the sidewalk, so my father brought out several of those forbidding chairs, barely softened by the frilly cushions my mother had crocheted. The grown-ups sat on them, and our Tía Keka showered her cousin Juan with questions. In a voice he tried to keep calm, Juan told her how the folks of Brač[14] were getting poorer and poorer; how the vines were yielding less and less and how the olive groves produced smaller and smaller olives; how the war had embittered everyone, because there wasn't a family that had not lost a son or, even worse, did not have to take care of an invalid.

At one point his eyes filled with tears and he remained silent, while Mama and Tía Keka sighed and exclaimed almost simultaneously, "Holy Mother of God!"

I looked at my father. Removed from all of us, he glumly chewed on his cigar. This powerful man, too, was

---

[14] One of ten larger Dalmatian Islands located off the port of Split.

on the verge of tears. He got up abruptly and went indoors.

None of this made sense to us children. The younger ones ran around playing tag. My older cousin, the one with the long trousers, challenged me to a race, and off we went, down the street. When the race ended in a tie, my cousin claimed that the tight-fitting long johns he was forced to wear had prevented him from being the undisputed victor.

Later we played ball. The game was closely watched by our mothers, who were probably thinking about the work facing them that night: cleaning and ironing our sailor suits to make them presentable the following Sunday.

***

At four we were all seated around the table for the important hour of afternoon coffee. The tablecloth, as resplendently white as an altar cloth, almost disappeared under the flowery cups, the big breadbasket in the center, and half a dozen dishes and trays holding biscuits, *pršurate, hrštulas,*[15] a gigantic strudel, rhubarb jam, and a cake decorated with shredded coconut and multicolored candy.

---

[15] *Pšurate*: round fritters made with mashed potatoes, grated apples, flour, raisins, prunes, walnuts, orange peels, cinnamon, brandy, and malt liquor. *Hrštule*: knot-shaped fritters made with eggs, sugar, flour, and either vanilla or liquor.

We, the sailors, felt our uniforms demeaned when our mothers, to prevent cocoa stains from ruining the outfits, insisted on tying vulgar square bibs around our necks. That's when my older cousin adjusted his tie and looked at me insultingly. But oh, divine justice! He would be the only one to get slapped that day for having dirtied the lapel of his brand-new suit jacket. Now *I* was entitled to a mocking smile, but I preferred to pretend this was not my concern and to keep on stuffing myself and guzzling cocoa like the rest of the kids. Meanwhile the adults drank coffee and chatted animatedly.

Clearly, Tío Juan was the guest of honor. At a certain moment, he got up ostentatiously and, with unexpected speed, limped to his room, at the end of the passageway, near the pantry at the far end of the house. He came back with the little package I recognized: the almond sweets. Emptying them on the table, he said in his language (the same language we prayed in every night), "That's all I have left."

In one instant Tío Juan had become the poorest man in the world. But did we care? It was much too enjoyable to be chewing on those sweets and, in the end, to come up with a whole almond.

***

For us children the next few days went by with unaccustomed rapidity: we gulped down our meals in a hurry, made short shrift of our homework, and barely went outside to play with the neighborhood kids. Tío Juan had become the center of all our curiosity and fantasy. A good narrator, he kept telling his sister about the many events that had occurred in her native village since she had left it fifteen long years ago, about the vineyards, the olive groves, and so on and so on. The war had been the worst of it. In Pučišća, as in all villages of Brač, even boys of sixteen were drafted into the army. Many of them did not return and lay buried under wooden crosses in foreign lands. Others, like him, had been luckier. They were wounded at the outset of the conflict and became prisoners of the French. Walking with a limp, or even losing an arm, was a small price to pay for staying alive.

Many nights I heard the roar of cannons and the explosion of grenades and saw soldiers die the way a boy imagines that soldiers die: with the flag raised on high, uniform buttons polished, a red spot over their hearts. Upon awakening, I heard the uneven gait of my uncle and recalled what he had said about the fleas and the rats, which ate them alive in the trenches, and at that moment war no longer seemed so glorious.

Sometimes, after lunch, my father and Tío Juan would get entangled in an exchange where the word "no" abounded and voices were raised. My mother would intervene on the pretext of having to clear the table, so the discussion would not turn into an argument. Papa, chewing on his cigar, would go off to the store. He'd sit down near the door on his massive chair and, unfolding his newspaper, would hold it so that it hid him completely. I wasn't all that sure that he was actually reading it; after all, he'd already read this same paper very early that morning.

Two weeks later Tío Juan moved to a boardinghouse, where he lived with fellow countrymen who were also fellow bachelors. He came to lunch the next Sunday. His expression, which normally tended to be somewhat sad, was radiant: he was to start work at the slaughterhouse the next day. My father remarked that the job was hard but that those who managed to get through the first week could earn a lot of money. It was work for young and strong people. My uncle was young. Papa toasted to him, wishing him good luck, and invited him to play boccie ball that afternoon.

I went with them. It was the first time my father had taken me to a gathering of grown-up men. Here was my chance to find out whether it was true! And it was. My father didn't disappoint me. Although Tío Juan and the others didn't do a bad job, there was no one capable of positioning the rolling ball close to the target jock, the *pollino*, with my Papa's precision. He made only one single mistake all afternoon; indeed, every time my father hit the ball of his opponent, he dislodged it so completely that the other player felt like giving up.

After interminably discussing each questionable move and calling down the power of all the saints of heaven in an uproar of shouts, the players fell completely silent the moment anyone was rolling a ball.

Suddenly something happened. One of the men watching the game whistled loudly, and, as if obeying a command, everybody left the court and went into the clubhouse. There they took their seats around a large table on which stood four enormous wine jugs and two long rows of glasses. The manager's wife brought me lemonade and made me sit off in a corner. The men gulped down a couple of drinks in almost total silence. Some were wiping the sweat off their faces, and all were grumbling. Then someone's fist came down so hard on the table that the wine made waves in the decanters. *"Bogami!"*

And they all started talking at the same time. From what I could tell, a group of Spaniards, headed by a certain Nicanor García, had been watching the game with binoculars from a two-story house on the next street. "Spying" was the word used. The matter was considered so reprehensible that all Spaniards from the king on down, all Spaniards born and to be born, would have trembled before the epithets launched against their respective mothers in a volley of shouts, in which one could make out curses and blasphemies. "Take it easy, take it easy," advised Don Pablo Drpić, a slight and nervous old man with white hair and dark eyes. "Keep calm, fellows. We have two possibilities. The first is to play badly on purpose; the other's to build a brick wall eight meters high."

"Shut up, old asshole!" shouted a youth called Frane.

The insult was too coarse, even considering the charged atmosphere in the clubhouse, and the old man got up livid, though composed: "If I were your age and had your strength, Frane, I would make you eat your words and your teeth. But I'll forgive you because you're young and foolish. What I want to say is simply this: you can't keep on training here within view of our rivals."

I looked at my father. The fizz of my lemonade was tickling my nose. Papa, having bitten off the tip of his new cigar and spat it out to one side, cleared his throat, lit up, exhaled a big mouthful of blue smoke, and said in a slightly tremulous voice: "Frane, first of all you're going to apologize to Don Pablo, or else... just bear in mind that what he can't do, I can do very well, if need be."

Frane, a tall, strapping guy, with curly blond hair covering his forehead, had a habit of moving his eyebrows in an odd manner. Getting up sheepishly, he stuttered: "Do-Don Pa-pa-blo, I'm so-sorry. I don't know wha-what I'm sa-saying."

"It's all right, son. I love you just as much as I do the rest of these fellows."

And the bitter smile of Don Pablo felt like a sort of benediction.

On the way home, my father did all he could to erase the impression I had received at the club; but when you're eight years old, words and gestures scar for life. For the first time I suspected that not all people were good.

I slept badly that night. I had a strange and distressing dream. A huge boccie ball came rolling downhill along the street, getting bigger and bigger until it became wider than the street itself and began to flatten the houses, crushing and absorbing them; finally, the street disappeared and the immense ball ended up in the sea with a tremendous splash that drenched the entire city.

I was woken by the sound of rain on the corrugated metal roof. The dawn was pale like the sad face of Don Pablo.

***

A day later, Papa brought home a huge fish, and my mother immediately started to prepare it in a special, rarely used pot. I knew that the next day we would have *polenta*[16] with marinated fish, a dish to make your mouth water or, according to the picturesque Adriatic expression, *maza la brada.*[17]

---

[16] Cooked coarse cornmeal porridge of Italian origin.
[17] Literally, "juice dripping down your chin."

Time rushed by. Each day was shorter and colder than the one before. We no longer could go outside in the afternoon to play ball or spin tops. In the morning the roofs were covered with hoarfrost, and the wooden curbs, edging the sidewalks, seemed equally white and slippery. Winter would soon set in, with the joy of snow and the sadness of thaws and mud.

Tío Juan came to our house almost every day. He had turned thinner and paler, and even his limp had become more pronounced. He was waiting for the answer to a letter he had sent to Europe, but the answer did not come.

He would sit down, depressed, next to the black stove and once in a while would utter some brief and sad comment. My mother would look at him with tenderness, shaking her head, disheartened.

When the store did not claim his attention, Papa would come into the kitchen and, without saying a word, put his powerful hand on our uncle's shoulder. At this Tío Juan would cheer up a bit and smile wanly. Mama would start singing an ancient song with her gentle, caressing voice, full of emotion:

"Sinoć si mi rekla da ljubiš samo mene.. ."

[Last night you told me you loved no one but me...]

Soon our uncle would join in, singing along softly, with tears in his eyes:

"Evo ti prsten raćam, što si mi na dar dala,
na kojem ti, malena, hvala, ljubav je prestala..."

[I'm returning the ring you gave me, my little darling,
I'm not grateful to you, now that love has vanished...]

And so the long harsh winter went by.

***

I did not know what a contract was until I saw Papa, Barba Jule, and Kum Grgo work on the road. In various carts, including the one belonging to Oyarzún, they hauled large quantities of stone and sand to the site. Toiling from sunup to sundown with picks and shovels, the men got a whole block ready. Using strings and levels they framed the sidewalks with long planks. They stopped work only briefly to have lunch; then, each equipped with a bottle of wine mixed with water, they continued their labor until nightfall. At the end of a day's work they put the tools away in a large lockbox, which was left in the middle of the street, and placed a lit lantern on top of it to warn the public that the road remained closed to traffic. Barba Jule and Kum Grgo went downhill to their families, and Papa came home exhausted, dragging his feet.

The contract with the city stipulated that the work was to be finished in one month, and Papa worried that the days were still too short and the weather too unstable. "If it doesn't rain we can finish on time. Otherwise…"

For us kids it was fun to see them work; often, after school, we tried to help by lugging a few stones. My father and his two countrymen, kneeling and holding heavy hammers, arranged the stones on a bed of sand. Every so often they would stand up, not to rest, but rather to ram the cobblestones with extremely heavy logs of hardwood, which were equipped with two handles to enable two men to bear down simultaneously. In the meantime the laborers from Chiloé piled up more sand and more stones, as if they begrudged my father and his friends one minute's respite.

Every day, on arriving home, we saw the progress of the paving job; in the space of one week a whole block of cobblestones had been put down. Very soon after that, more than three blocks were ready. At that point, to save time, Papa decided that instead of eating at home, he would eat his lunch at the work site. So every day, on our way to school, we took him a pot wrapped in a white cloth, a loaf of fresh bread, and a bottle of wine, in addition to his obligatory ration of Tuscan cigars.

The contract was fulfilled exactly on time. One afternoon my father put on his Sunday best—watch chain draped across his chest, shoes well polished, and the tips of his moustache appropriately twisted—and went downtown, tightly holding onto his hat, so the wind, which was blowing in capricious gusts, would not rip it off his head. He was going to collect his hard-earned money.

That night the three partners, sitting in our kitchen, enjoying small glasses of *rakija* and some dried figs, divided up the money in three equal parts. Barba Jule said he would buy a horse to replace the old nag that was pulling his rental cab; Kum Grgo wanted to fix his place up a bit, to prepare for the possible courtships of his many daughters. My father had already decided to put in new floors throughout our house.

The newly paved street was inaugurated one Sunday at noon to the sounds of a band. Several gentlemen with top hats and double-breasted frock coats, accompanied by ladies in wide-brimmed hats, arrived by "motor car." All the neighbors came out to look, most of them secretly hoping to see the car roll downhill. But this did not happen, even though the machine had been left unattended. Its driver, with visor cap and safety glasses ("chauffeur" was the word I learned that day), had gone off to get a closer view of the dedication. In this ceremony a lady—wearing long gloves adorned by a row of diminutive buttons—used tiny gold scissors to cut a tricolor silk ribbon that had been stretched across the brand-new stone pavement. My father stood close by and answered the questions put to him by one of the dignitaries.

The playing of the band livened things up, and people were talking and shouting greetings to each other. One of the gentlemen—the mayor—took off his shining top hat, got a piece of paper out of his pocket, and began to read a speech. His words were whipped away by the breeze, which was becoming a whistling wind. My father looked up, and I followed his glance. Dark clouds were skimming across the sky and soon covered the sun. A strong gust of wind sent one of those elegant hats rolling along on the ground. Suddenly the squall struck.

At first there were snowflakes, then hail, and, after that, a downpour that scattered the entire crowd in seconds. The orator put away his speech and made for the car, gallantly allowing several ladies to precede him while he got pelted by the cloudburst; the huge drops of rain sonorously bounced off his top hat. The chauffeur put on his glasses and tried to start the motor. The motor spluttered once or twice, then stalled. No matter how hard the man cranked the handle, making the vehicle sway in the process, the car refused to budge. Pushing the curtains aside, the mayor stuck his head out and asked for a push. The driver leaped into his seat, and my father and his partners pushed until the motor started with uneven explosions. The car went downhill, bouncing over the recently inaugurated pavement. The rest of the official party climbed into their vehicles, and soon the rain had swallowed up the caravan. My father threw away his soggy cigar, burst out laughing, and, cramming on his hat, came to take me by the hand.

We arrived home soaked to the skin; a carefully prepared Sunday lunch was waiting for us. My father explained the roles of the mayor, governor, commissary of police—in short, of all the officials we had just encountered in that ill-fated ceremony. The event would be permanently etched in our minds, down to such details as the musicians' rain-filled instruments and the dark color of their uniforms leaking onto their red collars and cuffs.

During the afternoon there were two or three more squalls, each one shorter than the preceding one, and around four o'clock the sun was shining once more. People came to take a look at the new street, and kids were running all over the place. My father, sitting by the entrance to his store, took stock of his work without hiding his pride and released big puffs of smoke. Some of the passersby stopped briefly to chat with him. At about six Barba Jule and Kum Grgo showed up with their respective families: the girls bedecked with ribbons and frills, the boys with starched collars and bow ties, except for the youngest ones (in sailor suits, of course). The adults went indoors and left us to play tag and "cops and robbers" in the street.

It rained heavily that night; my father got up very early to check on how well the water was running along the gutters of the new street. Judging by the naughty little tune he sang as he was shaving, he was very pleased with his inspection.

A few days later the three partners had secured a new contract, this time to lay down a stone pavement in a distant section of town near the beach. They bought oxen and carts and hired many laborers. Papa offered to teach Tío Juan the trade, an offer the latter accepted gladly: only in this way could he save the money he needed to return to his homeland.

Once again Tío Juan came to live with us, although we saw very little of him because he and Papa got up at the crack of dawn and didn't return until nightfall, when we children were already in bed. Only on Sundays did we go for a walk, invariably ending with my father's inspection of the work site. There, in the middle of the street, under a tent next to the gigantic toolbox, was Oyarzún, the cart driver, who was admirably suited for his new role as *guachimán.*[18]

The Chiloé islander prepared *café carretero.* He boiled water in a small pot over an open fire, threw in two enormous spoonfuls of ground coffee, and let the mixture simmer for a while. Next he removed the pot from the fire

---

[18] Corruption of the English term "watchman."

and, taking a burning log, immersed it briefly in the brew. After the coffee grounds sank to the bottom, Oyarzún carefully poured the black liquid into some chipped enamel mugs. Everyone added sugar to taste, and it turned out to be delicious! My mother wouldn't have allowed me to have any, of course, but my father was teaching me how to be a man.

On the way home I asked many insistent questions, but received only vague answers from my father. Tío Juan smiled and talked little, but his limp seemed slighter.

The new pavement contract, too, was a success, and Tío Juan found himself the owner of a fat wad of bills, which he counted twice under the store's paraffin lamp.

One Saturday, as we were finishing lunch, Papa and our uncle decided to take everybody for a boat ride on the bay. In our excitement, we acted so wild that our mother intervened with uncustomary energy. Realizing that we might not be allowed to go, we quickly calmed down and were soon marching downhill, as always, clustered around my father's imposing figure.

We walked to the beach along streets I didn't know. Next to the water we saw a line of boats turned on their sides on the sand. Papa examined each of them and picked out the best one, although to me they all seemed the same. He spoke to the owner, a plump and gesticulating Spaniard who launched at least three thundering curses before closing the deal. My father checked out the oars with the air of an expert, showing off a bit, and at last the three men pushed the boat into the water.

It was the first time I had seen the city from the sea; in fact, it was my very first boat ride. Yet this trip didn't seem strange to me at all. I was used to hearing my father tell about his past maritime adventures, so riding in a boat on a calm spring afternoon was something I had already done a thousand times in my imagination. Perhaps the only novelty was the squeaking of the oarlocks and the splashing of the water against the blades of the oars.

We passed a ship lying silently at anchor. It looked as tall as the mansions surrounding the square but smoke had dirtied it, and filth was pouring out of openings in its side. It was a *caponero*, a ship that came every year to pick up meat from the refrigerating plant. From this close, this ship seemed very different from the way it appeared to me every morning when I walked down the hill on my way to school. Gulls hovered nearby, alighting lazily on the greenish water.

I looked toward the city. Rows of one-storied houses climbed a gentle slope in a great open semicircle, and from them emerged a group of very high and beautiful buildings: the ones surrounding the square, and those along Roca Street, which led down to the sea... Farther back, the hill, with its iron cross—the Cerro de la Cruz—and more and more one-storied, red-roofed houses, painted in many different colors, in all some twenty blocks wide and about eight or ten blocks deep. The streets were wide and straight: Paraguaya, Boliviana, Independencia, Balmaceda, Errázuriz, Roca, Waldo Seguel, Valdivia,[19] Colón, Ecuatoriana,[20] Mejicana, Progreso,[21] Sarmiento... Piers jutted into the sea: for passengers, the "green" pier so well known to us, and then the two piers for cargo, gray, covered with coal dust, with rails that carried steam-operated cranes and hopper cars... and farther on, warehouses upon warehouses with large letters on their roofs: Menéndez Behety, Braun and Blanchard, Stubenrauch & Co. Beyond them, to the north and to the south, empty beaches and, at some distance in either direction, the dry docks, where shored-up ships had turned into strange structures lying at the mouth of rivers, lifeless, their boilers cold.

My father said it was a beautiful city, and for the first time Tío Juan agreed. They rowed slowly toward the beach. You could see the sandy bottom through the

---

[19] Now "José Menéndez."
[20] Now "Ignacio Carrera Pinto."
[21] After World War II named "Yugoslavia", now "Croatia."

green water, and to our utter amazement, huge shoals of fish swam by.

***

How many days we had to talk and fantasize! How marvelous was the sea, which had unveiled for us the essence of our land!

Those hills we gazed at that evening, as the sun set them aglow with red, purple, and violent orange, now seemed closer to us, more our own. Oh, what a beautiful land God had given us!

2

THE UNKNOWN BROTHER

Although my father had clearly explained the whole matter to us and we all knew that we had an older brother—the son of his first marriage, which had taken place in Dalmatia—we were amazed when we saw the recent arrival. Tall, solid, gray-eyed, with long curls escaping from under his hat, he looked every inch a man. He wore strange wide trousers, tucked into short crushed-leather boots and held up by a wide, embossed leather belt decorated with silver buttons and fastened by a large buckle. Stuck in this belt in back, he had a large knife with a bone handle in a silver-tipped sheath. He carried a revolver on his hip, a guitar slung over his shoulder, and a white silk kerchief tied around his neck.

"Nice-looking *pibes,*"[22] said that strange brother of ours in his odd way of talking.

"He's a gaucho,"[23] explained my father.

---

[22] Argentine term for "boys."

My mother gave him a hug and invited him to sit down and have a cup of coffee with us. There were sweets and a cake, just as on holidays, but he barely took a nibble. Nobody knew what to say during that first strained encounter. Finally my father led him to a room in the rear of the house, across from Tío Juan's, and left him there.

We soon forgot about the recent arrival and went out into the street to play. After all, he hadn't brought us any candy, not even a goat cheese.

But at seven the next morning, we awoke to the strumming of a guitar and a man's voice singing sentimentally:

"Vidalitá, ay, vidalitá
un amor y una pena, vidalitái... "[24]

The life of the entire family changed. Our gaucho brother got up before dawn to heat his *pava*[25] and brew himself a few *mates*.[26] Then, to start the day in

---

[23] Argentine cowboy.

[24] A refrain occurring in certain types of Argentine folk songs—usually a sad love song. "Vidalitá" sometimes also refers to this type of song itself.

[25] Kettle.

[26] Tea, made from dried leaves of mate, an herb, grown especially in Paraguay, Northern Argentina and Brazil, popular in South America. It is brewed in an often elaborately decorated gourd—also called mate—and sipped with a silver straw called a *bombilla* that has an in-built strainer on its lower tip.

earnest, he went out into the courtyard in his shirtsleeves to split wood; soon he was lending a hand with everything. He was a good workman, cheerful and industrious. He learned how to lay pavement and stayed abreast of my father, lining up rocks and ramming them into the ground. He cooked lunch over a fire built in the street, and, of course, brewed himself a few more *mates*. Sundays at dawn he harnessed the oxen and took his cart to the nearby forest to fetch firewood. In the afternoons he either strummed his guitar, singing in his deep, moving voice, or gave us detailed accounts of his Patagonian adventures.

My father called our unknown brother Viekoslav, but he asked to be called Lucho. He had largely forgotten his native Dalmatian tongue and spoke Spanish peppered with gaucho idioms. Almost every sentence included the word *che*;[27] to him, we kids were *pendejos*, young ladies *pibas*, little girls *pebetas*, my mother *la Vieja*, and my father, of course, *el Viejo*.

He would boast: "When I get hold of a *piba, che*, I make her remember what a *gringo*[28] is like, I sure make her remember!" And his deep voice trailed off in a singsong that we found very funny.

---

[27] A word—often used as an exclamation in colloquial speech—meaning "man" in Mapundungun, the native language of the Mapuche Indians, original inhabitants of Central Chile.
[28] Here, any fair, light-skinned person of European descent.

Lucho and Tío Juan soon became inseparable; at times they woke me when they came in late at night, tiptoeing along the passageway to their rooms. Two doors squeaked slightly, boots thudded to the floor, and mattress springs creaked; I might hear a half-suppressed cough and then silence.

Some afternoons and on holidays Lucho and I went for long walks. Occasionally all of us boys latched onto his arms, just as we did with our father. Lucho's curiosity propelled us along every street of the city. That's how we got to know our two rivers, the Río de las Minas and the Río de la Mano.[29]

The city developed northward toward the Río de las Minas, the larger of the two. This river came by its name from the gold placers that had capriciously altered the riverbed from the river's source down to the outskirts of town; from the coal seams visible on its banks; and, not least, from the assertions of a "deluded" Frenchman who claimed that by merely digging a bit here and there, one could make jets of oil pour out of the nearby hills.[30]

The Río de la Mano, a mere stream running in a deep canyon, limited the city's growth to the south. It was considered unimportant except for the legend that gave birth to its name. Old-timers claimed that after the

---

[29] *Mina* is Spanish for "mine"; *mano* is Spanish for "hand."
[30] The Magellan region did turn out to be rich in oil, but this was not discovered till much later, on December 29, 1945.

departure of the garrison of Fort Bulnes—the bastion that had established Chilean sovereignty over the Magellan Strait when the city was founded—one of the Indian scouts was accused of stealing the chalice from the chapel. Local military justice decreed that the Indian's right hand be cut off and buried near the stream. But the severed hand did not bleed, nor did it decay; and however often the soldiers attempted to cover it with sand and rocks, it kept rising to the surface. This phenomenon inspired terror; soon not even the bravest dared to go near the place. Finally, one day, when the new settlement had been firmly established, the chalice turned up among the military baggage. Realizing that he had punished an innocent man, the garrison's commander, accompanied by the chaplain, went in search of the Indian, who was hiding out in the hills. Just as the hand did not bleed when it was cut off, so it was reattached to the wrist without leaving even a trace of a scar. Since then the stream was called Río de la Mano. Not a very original name, to be sure.

The Río de las Minas was different. Although it normally carried little water, the spring thaw and every downpour turned it into a muddy torrent; and because the surrounding land was flat, the river left its bed and inundated the city's entire coastal district, flooding houses and threatening to carry them out to sea. The fire brigade would then ring its persistent warning bell.

Every time a flood occurred, my father made Tío Juan and Lucho get up at daybreak. The three of them, in heavy overcoats and tall fisherman's boots, tossed empty sacks into a cart and took off for the beach. A couple of hours later they returned with a load of firewood and coal. The turbulent river, as it passed the Menendez Behety Company's Loreto mine, swept tons of coal along its path. That lost treasure belonged to anyone who had courage enough to wrest it from the sea.

The men came home soaked to the skin and frozen to the marrow; Mama welcomed them with huge mugs of coffee and a bottle of *rakija*. Their strength recovered, they unloaded the cart. They piled tree trunks and branches in one corner of the courtyard and—under a zinc lean-to, next to the storage shed—built a black mound with the coal.

On one such occasion my father remarked that we had enough coal for three months and enough firewood for at least two. In monetary terms this represented a small fortune, albeit soon to be transformed into smoke and short-lived heat.

***

Viekoslav-Lucho, quite apart from his role as our brother, was destined to cause some excitement. Good-looking, though rough-mannered, with his steely gray eyes and well-shaped nose, he became the center of attention for the opposite sex. His gaucho garb (which he didn't want to give up), his swinging gait, his long, curly hair—all aroused the curiosity of our female relatives. However, Lucho seemed more interested in his guitar.

One day Kum Grgo came over to talk to my father. In the space of three long hours, they drank up three big jugs of good wine. And every time we children tried to peek in the dining room, our mother peremptorily shooed us away.

As a result of this visit, Papa took Lucho to Stubenrauch's the next day and brought him back home laden with packages. Papa then made our big brother sit on a chair in the middle of the kitchen and put a towel around his neck. Knowing what was expected of her, Mama took a comb and a pair of scissors and proceeded to cut Lucho's tangled mane with a dexterity derived from years of practice on our young heads. Our brother emerged from this procedure more Viekoslav than Lucho, looking amazingly like my father, thirty years younger and thirty kilos lighter. He kept rubbing his neck, exclaiming, "Darn! How cold it feels!" He then took himself off to his room, while my father lit the umpteenth cigar of the day.

Mama got supper ready. We sat down at the table, but Lucho didn't show up. At a sign from my father, Tío Juan went to fetch him, his uneven steps echoing along the passageway. He soon returned, accompanied by the creaking of new shoes. The tall figure of our gaucho brother appeared in the doorway. Dressed in a dark suit, with sleeves a bit too short for him and a showy tie, the cuffs of his shirt covering half his hands and with gray leggings over his patent-leather shoes, he looked like a gentleman's understudy, ill at ease. With an embarrassed smile he remarked, "To heck with these tight pants. They're going to split as soon as I sit down; they're going to split for sure!"

He was uncomfortable throughout dinner. The collar bothered him; he kept pulling at the tie until it looked like tripe. He loosened his belt and finally, in despair, took off his jacket. My mother smiled tolerantly, while my father remained serious as a statue.

Lucho-Viekoslav suffered; but seeing that nobody was willing to pity him, he decided to make a joke of the matter: "This is just like when they dressed me up as a sergeant in the Argentine pampa."

The next day, when I came home from school, Lucho was waiting for me. It was quite obvious that Mama had put lot of work into lengthening the sleeves of his jacket and shortening those of his shirt. His ironed tie looked as good as new. Lucho was busy giving shape to his new hat. It was black, of course, because Papa wouldn't approve of any other color. I hurried to get ready and we set out.

The afternoon was mild and calm. There wasn't even a breeze. The neighborhood women and little kids were watching from their front doors or their windows. The bigger boys played ball in the street. Lucho and I climbed to the top of the Cerro de la Cruz. The city was a truly beautiful sight. Before us lay a grid of straight streets. A few had stone pavement, but most were unpaved, flanked by shallow gutters. Closest to us was the broad Avenida Libertad,[31] then, getting ever nearer to the sea, followed Talca,[32] Chiloe, Bories, and Magellan Streets and some others whose names I can't recall. To the left flowed the winding Río de las Minas. Above the red roofs of the pastel-colored houses curled plumes of kitchen smoke; farther off, the beach stretched in a wide arc, festooned by the white garland of the waves. Some dozen large ships and countless schooners, launches, and small craft dotted the bay. We could see the three piers.

In the distance, beyond the Strait, we could make out a bluish strip: the low hills of Tierra del Fuego. On the horizon to the extreme right rose a mountain with two white peaks disappearing into the clouds: Mt. Sarmiento. According to my father, if Mt. Sarmiento wasn't shrouded in clouds, you could be quite sure the dreaded southern gale would start blowing the following day.

---

[31] Now "Avenida España."
[32] Now "Alvaro Sanhueza."

Lucho and I spent a long while enjoying the view. Finally my newly found brother took me by the hand, and we walked downhill along a steep street. Minutes later we reached the square. There were many people milling about. Young ladies in huge hats with colored feathers, short veils down to their noses, gathered up their skirts a bit each time they stepped onto or down from the sidewalk, revealing boots with mother-of-pearl buttons. At the four corners of the square next to some squat cement columns where the leading department stores posted bright announcements, groups of men had congregated. Their sole occupation was to look at the ladies, and every few moments they doffed their hats to nod a greeting.

Lucho joined one of the groups, so I felt free to check on what was happening to the statue of Ferdinand Magellan. It was surrounded by tall scaffolding, covered with canvas and mats. In the middle, also covered with sacking, there appeared to be a kind of tower. But just then the military band got ready to play in the gazebo. I hurried over and ran into a number of friends from school. It was almost dark when Lucho, very worried, found me and rushed me home at a trot. We made it just in time for supper.

Many days went by. The year was drawing to a close. We went to bed at nine, but daylight filtered through the shutters, so it was difficult to fall asleep. We took up our game of hopping from bed to bed until one night, when the rumpus got out of hand, we broke a box spring. The ensuing scolding was such that we gave up this diversion for good. We had to get used to covering our heads with our blankets to create darkness.

A second inauguration ceremony was held to celebrate the newly paved streets. The gentlemen sported the same frock coats; the mayor drove up in the same automobile and, of course, brought the same speech that got rained out previously. This time there was also a popular fiesta with a roast on the spit, guitar playing, and singing. Mama fetched us away when the entertainment was at its height. Papa came home much later in a very cheerful mood. From our beds we listened for a long while to the songs my father was determined to teach Lucho and Tío Juan.

***

It was Christmas Eve. Our teacher, Señorita Julia, had decorated our little school with oak branches and little colored flags. She made us sing the songs she had patiently taught us during the last two years. Then she handed out our certificates, and to those like me, who were not coming back the following year,[33] she gave medals of the Virgen del Carmen[34] and kissed us on the

---

[33] The novel takes place in the Southern Hemisphere, so it is summer at Christmas time and the end of the school year.
[34] Patron saint of Chile.

forehead. I tried to thank her, as my father had instructed me to do, but, seeing tears in her eyes, I didn't dare say anything. We came home in a buzz of excitement: our vacations had begun! No more getting up at the crack of dawn, no more homework, no more shoe shining, no more bookbags. Mama was frantically busy at the oven and with the frying pans, concocting cakes, pies, and buns. Our mouths were watering.

Papa, Tío Juan, and Lucho, who had gone off early with one of the carts, returned with a load of firewood. On top of it they had tied a small live oak tree. Planted in a tub wrapped in a red piece of cloth, it was soon covered with shining red, green, blue, silver, and gold balls, packets of candy, and chocolates in aluminum foil; there was even a real bird's nest from the forest, perched on one of its branches. It contained three tiny green speckled eggs.

In the afternoon Mama gave us an early supper and sent us off to our room. For a while we somewhat cautiously played at hopping from bed to bed, but in the end we got tired and fell asleep.

Close to midnight Papa and Mama had a hard time shaking us awake. In a daze I got up and went to the dining room. There was the tree, in a glory of candles; Tío Juan, with a sad look on his face; and Lucho, strumming his guitar. Mama began singing:

"U ponoć se Bog rodi,
Nebo i zemlju prosvitli."

[At midnight, when God was born,
He illuminated Heaven and Earth.]

My father solemnly untied five candy packets from the tree and gave one to each of us. The table was loaded with delicacies. Yawning and tossing my head to stay awake, I tasted the strudel, the *pršurate,* and the cake and sipped a cup of cocoa. Firecrackers went off in the street, and the sound of church bells came from a great distance. Jesus was born.

Lucho plucked his guitar strings, searching for the melody, and Mama and her brother once more intoned:

"At midnight, when God was born
He illuminated Heaven and Earth."

***

To visit one's godfather on Christmas Day was a sacred duty. There were five of us, so there were five godfathers to be greeted: Kum Nikola, Barba Jule, Kum Jakov, Kum Grgo, and Kum Petar. In every house we were offered candies, chocolates, cake, macaroons, and the usual Dalmatian delicacies, even a small a glass of port. Grannies and aunts, bustling about their kitchens just like Mama, showered us with kisses. We shook hands with shy little girl cousins in starched dresses and ribbons in their hair and, as we walked by, got a few surreptitious kicks from our boy cousins, who had as little use for us as we had for them. At several of our stops we managed to play a while, but our cousins also had to visit their godfathers, so the whole morning was spent in hellos and goodbyes. Christmas morning was rather hard work.

Papa, too, had to make the rounds and was received with *rakija*, figs, nuts, raisins, and fritters; in turn, he needed to be home to welcome his own guests, so everybody was engaged in a race against time. Returning home, Papa found several friends and relatives waiting for him: Barba Pave, the baker Don Pedro, the Galician greengrocer Don Gabriel, Barba Marko, Kum Jose, Kum Ivon (nicknamed "Black Cat"), and old Oyarzún, his inevitable cigar-stub protruding from under his limp moustache. My father played the host cheerfully and treated his visitors with sincere affection. Our dining room resounded with laughter and jokes. Sweets, laboriously prepared by Mama and enthusiastically praised by the guests, were gulped down with alarming rapidity. Dishes were emptied and replenished again and again. Glasses of port and brandy clinked.

"It's Christmas, after all!"

"Salud!"

"Cheers!"

"Nazdravlje!"

"Salú!"

"To your health!"

Eventually Oyarzún rose lazily, and the others, too, realized it was time to leave. Papa saw them to the door. There they chatted a little longer. Finally, slightly tipsy, they went off in various directions.

In the afternoon, our parents took us for a walk around the square and along the principal downtown streets. The windows of the big stores were lit up and exquisitely decorated with Christmas motifs. Then we entered the cathedral to take a long look at the Nativity. It seemed to me that the Christ Child was very large compared to his mother.

***

The week between Christmas and New Year was undoubtedly when we had the most fun. It was daylight until about eleven o'clock at night, and we had no reason whatsoever to turn in early, so we played in the street until late. Even Papa liked to kick our ball, taking good care that it did not land on the head of any of his youthful adversaries. We flew kites, set off firecrackers, and released balloons into the breeze. We admired the clouds glowing red-violet, blue, and yellow, long after the sun had slowly disappeared behind the mountains. We watched the immense reddish disk of the moon rise from the sea and, as it gradually turned pale, imagined that we saw on its surface the silhouettes of St. Joseph, the Virgin, and the Christ Child.

The night air was refreshing. The stars shone brilliantly. All were silver, except for one that was red. Papa said that was Mars. He then pointed out the five stars of the Southern Cross, the Three Marys, and many others. Finally he told us that far, very far beyond all this and keeping everything moving in its course was the master of the whole universe, who had created heaven and earth but who was also able to destroy it all with one single word. We felt in awe of God's presence.

I couldn't but help remembering right then the day I had killed a fly. My father took it, placed it under a magnifying glass, and told me to study it. He explained some things that I was barely able to comprehend, but I did understand that in the larger scheme of things, this fly was as important as a human being, because in order to survive, it too needed air, soil, and nourishment. Like us, it was God's creature, and although it might seem useless to us, it unquestionably had some purpose—if nothing more than to keep people awake with its annoying buzzing.

New Year's Eve was always marvelous, but this year it was better than ever because Papa decided we could stay up. Tío Juan, who was with us in the street, marveled at the mildness of the night and the balminess of the air. He told us, partially in his own language and partially in broken Spanish, how back home his people would now be suffering from the bitter cold, eating biscottis and drinking *rakjia* and *prošek,* close to the *komin,*[35] until the stroke of midnight, when it would be time to congratulate their grandfather; then they would all hurry off to bed to get warm. He recalled the lovely bay of Pučišća—Pučišća vala (which had even inspired a romantic ditty), where the foam splashing against the rocky shore would turn to ice and where one could hear a joyous pealing of bells from the beautiful belfry. But all of these memories were so very distant, so very far, far away.

"Tamo daleko, daleko, kraj mora
tamo je selo moje, tamo je ljubav moja..."

[There far, far away, by the sea
There is my village, there is my love...][36]

When night finally fell, putting an end to our games, silence and darkness surrounded us, except for the intense glimmer of my father's cigar. Suddenly the first detonations resounded. We saw a red streak rise over the sea. A shower of fireworks invaded the sky and

---

[35] Fireplace.
[36] This song is considered the anthem of Dalmatian immigrants to the Americas.

extinguished the stars, turning night into day. We heard the church bells ring out once or twice, only to be immediately drowned out by the firecrackers and the sirens of the boats anchored in the bay. People ran out of their houses to embrace and wish each other a Happy New Year. We children ran from door to door to greet our playmates. All this uproar and the brilliant lights dimming the stars may have lasted five or ten minutes or an hour, but it overwhelmed my senses. As suddenly as it had begun, the hubbub ceased. A smell of smoke filled the air. That was all... or maybe not! Perhaps the stars had become more brilliant.

We were sitting around the table when Lucho turned up. He'd been in the square and returned delighted. A band of musicians had played in the gazebo and there had been dancing. He had received several unexpected and pleasant *abrazos*,[37] and some new friends had invited him for a drink in a bar. By then sleep got the better of us children and Mama just about had to carry us, one by one, to our beds.

***

Lunchtime was about as important as mass. No one started eating unless everyone was seated at the table. It was the moment for relaxed give-and-take, for banter, for jokes and even occasional snide remarks—

---

[37] Hugs.

usually about the daughter of some relative or acquaintance. My father was a hearty eater and enjoyed a leisurely conversation. We could all talk freely. Lucho and Tío Juan asked many questions; they wanted to know about the city and its inhabitants.

Papa told them that Punta Arenas was a new city and had been a penal colony until recent times. It had seen two terrible riots, real small-scale revolutions, bloody and useless. In one of those uprisings the governor and the priest had been killed and other atrocities committed. Papa would not talk about them in front of us. The cross on the hill was erected precisely to commemorate one of those violent episodes, and a legend woven around them asserted that a *caudillo*,[38] a Lieutenant Cambiazo, had buried a huge treasure somewhere near the beach and that whoever found it would become extremely wealthy.

"Many are still hunting for this treasure, but I have mine right here," concluded my father, glancing at my mother and us.

Tío Juan lowered his eyes and murmured, "And I left mine back home."

"'Cheers!" said my father, raising his glass.

"Uzdravlje!" replied Tío Juan, smiling sadly.

---

[38] Rebel leader.

3

REVEILLES AND TAPS

She was a very pretty little girl in a white dress with an embroidered collar, white socks, patent leather shoes, a large red silk ribbon in her hair, corkscrew curls down to her shoulders, blue eyes, and a little beauty spot on her left cheek. Her name was Antonia and she was pale. She had a blonde doll that closed its eyes when you put it down. The doll's eyes made a clicking sound, which Antonia's did not.

When she came with her mother—a pleasant, talkative lady—I kept my distance; but my father made me say hello to her and told me to take her out into the street to play with us. We actually had to teach her how to kick a ball. That's what caused the trouble. Running between our sallies, she fell and scraped her nose on the pavement. She burst out crying. There was nothing for it... we had to take her to her mother. The kind lady made light of the mishap, and soon, through her tears, the lovely Antonia tried to smile. She seemed comical with her scraped nose and her tiny beauty spot; still, we felt sorry for her.

That night I dreamed Antonia was an angel with large white wings, a huge golden bow in her hair. With that scraped little nose of hers, she kept fluttering around for a long time, buzzing like a fly. Her wings stirred up a breeze; they crackled like the sheets hanging on our clothesline. The breeze made me feel chilly. I woke up to find the wind whistling outside and icy air blowing in through a chink in the window.

***

It was one of those fierce storms that seemed about to send the whole city flying into the sea. My father was afraid to open the shutters facing the side from which the wind was blowing. He secured the patio door with heavy logs of firewood. No one dared venture outside without goggles to protect their eyes from the dust and sand bombarding the walls of the house. Once again our stovepipe turned red, bellowing like a blowtorch. Frigid air penetrated every corner. Doors and windows rattled as if they were about to be ripped off by the furious gale.

Not a soul made it to the *boliche* all morning; no one wanted to risk crossing the street. From the kitchen window I watched the chickens, barely able to stand, their feathers in disarray. Grains of corn were swept across the patio; the dog whined piteously in his doghouse.

Farther away, in the vegetable patch, the cabbage heads kept hitting the ground, and the rosebushes, on which Mama lavished such great care, quivered, as if someone were trying to uproot them.

Don Pedro Kuzmanić, the baker, fought his way through the cyclone and managed to reach our house. He had to leave his cart one street below ours. He carried the five kilos of bread—his customary noontime delivery to our store—in a basket hanging from his arm. His wasn't the bread we would eat, but it helped us to have ours.

Don Pedro was not only our parents' special friend, he was ours as well. He usually brought hot buns for us kids, but the day of the storm, the buns had got cold and encrusted with grains of sand. Papa invited him into the kitchen and there they sat a long while talking by the fire, each slowly sipping a glass of wine. Mama was already setting the table for dinner when Don Pedro, smiling pleasantly, said goodbye, pulled his cap over his ears, put on his goggles and went outside, firmly holding on to the door that the storm was shaking violently.

Tío Juan was scared. He kept pacing back and forth, apprehensively looking at the windows and the ceiling; he turned pale every time an especially strong gust shook the house. My mother seemed calm, but her lips moved incessantly: she was praying. My father, too, appeared tense as if he were afraid of something. But nothing happened. At about five the storm began to abate; by six, it had died down completely. The rooster crowed and the dog barked with gusto. We heard the tinkle of the little bell at the door of the *boliche* and in came Oyarzún, cigarette stub stuck to his lower lip, his nose purple, energetically rubbing his numbed hands.

The day was starting late, but start it did. In any case we knew the night would be tranquil and beautiful. Papa and Oyarzún had their brandy, talked as they always did, and in the end the cart-driver took off, silently and slowly, walking in front of his oxen, the cattle prod across his shoulder. He was indifferent to the passage of time; he counted the hours by the length of his own shadow. And so he lived from sunup to sundown, savoring every day of his life to the fullest.

It turned out to be a lovely night indeed. There were no sounds other than the barking of dogs, some very close by and piercing, others muted, at a great distance. Very far away, one could hear the mooing of cows, the bleating of sheep, and the plaintive *meee* of goats.

From below came the sound of the sea and the murmuring of the river; above us was the eternal twinkling of the stars. The full moon, as bright as day, sharply outlined the dark mountains behind the city.

Hooves clattered on the pavement, and the silhouette of the night watchman emerged from the shadows. He stopped at the corner and blew three short, clear notes on his whistle. Identical trills replied from far away. "All's well," explained my father. "Let's go to bed."

That night we didn't light the lantern we usually hung from the post by the door. The moonlight was bright enough.

***

There was a lot going on at the start of that year. Oyarzún announced he was marrying Calisto's widow, Hortensia, the cheerful washerwoman, whose fat and smiling daughter Rosalía occasionally helped my mother with the washing and ironing. Tío Juan had saved enough money to buy a return ticket to his Dalmatia and wanted to leave soon. Kum Jakov was pouring a cement floor in his butcher shop. Don Pedro, the baker, was looking forward to the birth of his first child. Kum Ivon, was planning to move into a new house. The Magellan Battalion was being expanded into a regiment, building new quarters on some abandoned pastures, high up on the outskirts of town—a turn of events that would be decisive for us.

We went to live in a different house, one on the corner just across from the future regimental headquarters. Two months of complete remodeling followed. A couple of Chilote[39] carpenters demolished

---

[39] Native of Chiloé.

walls, enlarged windows, built shelves, and installed electricity. There was an array of cables, switches, and fuses; finally bulbs were hung from red and yellow wires. The former *boliche* had become a real store. A colorful sign, Almacén Tres Estrellas (Three Stars Grocery), was painted above the double doors. We were about to begin a new life.

One morning soldiers drove a few heavy, horse-drawn carts up our street. By afternoon, we children had figured out how to tell a corporal from a sergeant, and a lieutenant from a captain.

The big carts kept rolling past, day after day. Their huge wheels clattered against the pavement as they were pulled uphill by powerful Friesians, sparks flying from their wide, shining hooves. Tarpaulins covered the loads of wood, bricks, and large cement barrels. Soldiers in gray uniforms with bright red decorations, wearing caps with broad red bands, walked on either side of the carts, shouldering their rifles. Whenever the troops marched by in the morning, or returned to their old barracks near the beach in the afternoon, curious faces appeared at windows and doorways.

Wooden barracks and large tents soon swallowed up the pastures. At night a few soldiers stood guard in front of a huge bonfire, while the rest of their unit slept in one of the big barracks.

Gradually the soldiers brought mules and cannons; they laid rails and began to level the terrain. Earth from the higher areas was loaded into handcarts and emptied onto the low-lying spots. Then walls rose up. You could already tell that it was an immense project.

We kids were fascinated by the goings-on, and our summer vacations that year turned out to be most entertaining. Not only did we watch the soldiers at work, listen to their snappy commands and, best of all, toward evening, enjoy the playing of the military band, but things were pretty lively at home too: the carpenters, my father, Tío Juan, and brother Lucho were all in a frenzy trying to get their job done in the least amount of time possible. From four o'clock in the morning, when the regimental bugler sounded reveille, to taps at nine o'clock at night, our lives and those of the soldiers ran a parallel course.

One Monday at 5 a.m. Papa threw open the double doors of his store. He claimed he was trying to get rid of the paint smell, but actually he was inaugurating the Three Stars Grocery. The term *boliche* had been banned from our vocabulary forever.

***

Just then, Oyarzún showed up. Papa filled two small glasses to the brim with *rakija* as always and was about to make a toast when an officer entered, followed by a sergeant. The sergeant took a few steps back. The officer approached the counter, leaning on it with gloved hands.

"Good morning, sir."

"Good morning, Captain."

"What makes you think I'm a captain?"

"The stars on your uniform," replied my father. "I served in the Austro-Hungarian Navy. I'm a seaman first class. I had three stars on my collar. That's why I named my grocery store the Three Stars." The captain proffered his hand; my father shook it respectfully. "At your service, Captain."

"We're raising a regiment. It'll take years and it'll keep on growing. For the time being I need a place where my men can buy a few things to eat, stuff to keep their uniforms clean, some fluid to shine their buttons, shoe polish, soap, and razor blades, in short... the basics. Could you stock some of those items?"

"I've already got all of them on hand. In addition, I also carry a great liniment for sore muscles."

The captain burst out laughing, and saluted smartly. My father clicked his heels and gallantly returned the military salute.

Oyarzún had been impatiently chewing his mustache and calmed down only after the departure of the captain and his escort. He raised his glass of *rakija*, downed it in one gulp, and observed: "Those army bucks! They're going to ruin the entire neighborhood. I bet you there won't be a healthy woman left around here… Damn it!"

***

The first Monday in March I started classes at the Colegio San José, run by the Salesian Brothers. I felt intimidated. Things were very different from the way they had been at Señorita Julia's little school. We had to line up in pairs and recite long prayers I didn't know. Only when the protracted assembly ended with an "Our Father" and a "Hail Mary" did I feel a bit more at ease: these were prayers I had learned from my first teacher.

The classrooms seemed immense and terribly cold. They had cement floors and huge, barred windows overlooking a central courtyard. The boys were fun, though. During the breaks we played ball, stalked around on stilts, rode the merry-go-round, or enjoyed the swings.

***

At school the priests in black—whom I was used to see emerging, frozen stiff, from their confessionals— were friendly and active. Some shot marbles; others played ball or tag right along with us, as if they themselves were kids. I soon knew their names: Father Torres; Father Re; the acolytes Olave and Andaur; Father Rojas; Father Fuenzalida, the director; Father Costamagna, and the teachers, Benove, Lagos, Salvetto, and Navarro. The latter didn't wear cassocks, but they too were somehow like priests. I didn't understand this very well at the beginning; it seemed to me that in a school run by priests, all teachers ought to belong to the clergy.

At least once a week, we went to church; the student body took up every bench, and even so, some of the bigger boys had to kneel in back, on the floor, for lack of space.

The school had a theater. Once a month we had a student show where we all performed, from the youngest, who recited poems from our reader, to the oldest, who painted on mustaches and beards with burned cork, dressed up as Romans, Chinamen, or whatever, and either made us laugh at their antics or moved us to tears with melodramas that always included a missionary with a long black woolen beard. In some skits the missionary converted the pagans and all ended well, but in others, he was mortally wounded by the "bad guy." As he lay dying, the "bad guy" would show up, full of remorse, and be pardoned by the moribund man of God "in the name of the Father, the Son and the Ho... ly... Gho... o... st." The "bad guy," by now converted into a "good guy," would say "Amen," and the curtain would fall while we wiped our noses.

On Sunday afternoons we had catechism and then the benediction at church, with lots of incense and chanting. A film at the school theater followed. It was right there that I saw my first movie: it was about an extremely comical man cranking the handle of a very odd automobile. The automobile took off on its own, scaring people, entering houses, going up and down stairways until, in the end, it crashed into a tree, whereupon its owner stomped on his hat in vexation.

***

Lucho and Tío Juan borrowed my books and locked themselves in the dining room. Tío Juan wanted to study Spanish; Lucho, wanted to improve his grammar. Sometimes they asked me questions I was unable to answer. In such cases they turned to my father, whom they never caught off guard: he had gone over the corresponding lesson very early in the morning, when we were still in bed.

***

About Lucho I can report that he very soon was able to write a letter to a girlfriend he remembered from the time they were, as he put it, "rolling in the bushes" near Santa Cruz, in the Argentine pampa. Tío Juan, on the other hand, got into a terrible mess with the language; he corrupted Spanish words, misled by Italian or French, not to mention his island dialect, complicated enough in itself. He argued about what he considered illogical rules and stubbornly defended terms of his own concoction.

Weeks flew by and the days became noticeably shorter. It got dark by seven. When we left for school in the morning, it was chilly, icy dew whitened the roofs and

- 85 -

the rising sun was a pale yellow disk. It was my job to accompany my brothers to Señorita Julia's before walking another four blocks to Colegio San José. At noon they were waiting for me, and together we walked uphill. As we climbed, the main gate of the regimental headquarters came into view, flanked by its crenellated towers and its enormous bronze cannon. A block away from home, we noticed our father waiting for us, his head surrounded by a little blue cloud of tobacco smoke. We ran to him. He made us look at the sea, pointing out the ships that were leaving or arriving, a schooner in the distance, a few launches coming and going between the larger boats.

"You'll be a sailor," he said to me one day, "a naval officer, not a simple seaman like me."

"Then you'll have to salute me."

"I'll be happy to, son. I'll be proud to."

My mother didn't like the idea. She had bad recollections of her long voyage from Genoa to Punta Arenas: two months spent on an old freighter, crowded with passengers, for whom she washed and ironed clothes to defray her expenses. There had been a violent storm off the Argentine coast, which forced the boat to take refuge in the Malvinas.[40] For her, one ocean voyage

---

[40] South American name of the Falkland Islands—a group of some two hundred islands about three hundred miles east of the Magellan Strait. The difference in names is not simply linguistic but also

was enough. No need whatsoever to defy the Almighty, who had given man land enough to live on.

Later, on the other hand, she would not object to one of my brothers joining the army; nor would she mind another son entering the priesthood... But then, a long time ago, a relative of hers had actually become nothing less than a bishop in Zagreb.

***

My father was a member of the Maritime Society and skipper of his rowing team. For that reason, once a week, when the team was training, he took off work at four in the afternoon and didn't return until dark. Sometimes he'd come home in a cheerful mood, other times he'd seem worried. Some holiday—I can't remember which one—was approaching and there was to be a rowing regatta. The Spanish team and teams from the navy and one or two sport clubs were good. Now Papa went daily to supervise our men.

One Sunday morning he took me along to Doberti's dry dock at the mouth of the Río de las Minas. There lay the boat, belly up, and four or five men were busily scraping and caulking it. About a dozen Dalmatians with carnations in the buttonholes of their Sunday suits looked on, offering advice. Don Simón Ružić was in charge of operations; he gave instructions in

---

political, involving the sovereignty of Argentina and the British Commonwealth.

his deep bass voice. My father took Don Simón aside. After a whispered conversation, both men carefully inspected the hull, sliding their fingertips over every joint of it, without missing a spot. Papa, using his carpenter's pencil, marked a number of places; I watched, not understanding what was going on. All the spots Papa marked were painstakingly recaulked. Hours crawled by. At last, the boat was ready to be painted. The crew applied an even, reddish color. By noon the first coat was done. Two men remained behind to stand guard. The rest of us went home for lunch. I was beginning to feel like a sailor.

We ate on the run. Papa barely said a word. Having eaten, he lit his cigar and took me by the hand, and off we went once more. It was a long haul: almost thirty blocks from our house on the hill down to those distant streets at the mouth of the river.

When we got there, the keel had a second coat of red paint and the men were beginning to apply white paint to the rest of the boat. For a while my father looked on in silence; then he started to inspect the paint job at close range, making numerous suggestions, until, at dusk, he was satisfied. "Slippery as a fish" was his assessment. That task completed, we stepped into the lean-to, where the oars were lying on special trestles. My father hefted each oar in turn, balancing it to find its center of gravity. He measured its length and scrutinized its blade; next, he penciled a number on every blade; last, he called the men one by one, assigned each of them an oar, and ordered them to line up for review.

"Stand straight! Hands at shoulder height! Oars touching the ground by your heels! Watch your alignment! Don't laugh, whatever you do! Look fierce! Chests out! Assholes tight! We have to scare the enemy from the outset. Now let's practice our battle cry: 'Ra, ra, ra, Chile and Dalmatia!'"

One crew member was not Dalmatian at all. He was a tousled, black-haired Hungarian with eyes clear as water and powerful muscles. He was the only one to wear his carnation not in his buttonhole but, instead, stuck behind his ear. Nonetheless, it was he who shouted the loudest: "Chile and Dalmatia!"

And so the Sunday of the regatta arrived. Papa went out at dawn. Mama stayed behind with our youngest brother, taking care of the kitchen and the grocery store, assisted by the fat Rosalía. Lucho, Tío Juan and the rest of us hurried down to the Green Pier. There was "Three Piers," the old cop, with his uniform, his dog, and a golden peaked helmet; the red cloth stars on his sleeve seemed bigger than usual, and his new shoes were shiny and creaked as he walked.

Leaning on the railing at the end of the pier, we looked northward to where the river flowed into the sea. In a short while, from behind the cargo piers, the white boat of the Maritime Society appeared, advancing slowly. My father, dressed in a blue jersey, stood at the stern while twelve oars moved rhythmically. When the boat was about a hundred meters away from the pier, the crew members raised the oars to a vertical position, so that they formed two perfect lines. My father maneuvered with the steering oar and the boat stopped sideways in the middle of the calm, green water. The others—the red boat of the Spaniards, a green boat from Club Victoria, a blue boat from the navy, and three more—formed a group. Oars on high, the crews gaily exchanged greetings.

Two revenue cutters, anchored close to the shore, sounded their sirens and hoisted bunting. The little multicolored flags fluttered in the wind. The captain of one of the revenue cutters addressed the crews through a megaphone: "Take position near the buoy marked by a red flag, a mile and half from the pier, close to the revenue cutter Yelcho.[41] Yelcho's commander will fire a pistol to start the race." Slowly the seven boats put out to sea. Yelcho, equally slowly, maneuvered until it had reached the buoy. We could barely make out the buoy, but we saw the boats line up, keeping a distance of some twenty meters from each other.

---

[41] The very same Yelcho which the saved Shackleton's South Pole expedition.

Near the pier two navy launches took their places, facing each other, each with an officer on board to indicate the finishing line. We had an ideal spot to see the end of the race, and my sailor hat felt like a ring of fire on my head.

"They're o-o-ff!" someone yelled.

A huge crowd was shoving against the railings of the pier, shouting encouragement to their team, although it was obvious that the crewmen were still too far out to hear them.

In consternation I watched the Spaniards' red boat take the lead, closely followed by the blue navy boat, the Victoria Club's green, and a yellow one from another club.

The white boat of the Maritime Society was trailing in the fifth spot. The Dalmatians were rowing with long, slow sweeps; all the others moved to a much faster beat.

All the ships' sirens began to wail. It was a noise both cheerful and penetrating, forcing you to stop up your ears. Reacting to the pulse of the short, strident whistles, the teams accelerated their pace, except for the Dalmatians, who were no doubt obeying the peremptory orders of their skipper, my father—stubborn old man that he was!

But by the time about a third of the course had been covered, the white boat had outstripped its green and yellow competitors. The crews of the red and blue boats tried to speed up, but the white boat was already on a level with the navy's blue. In a moment, the Dalmatians passed the navy boat. Now only the Spaniards were way ahead.

Their skipper, the redoubtable Nicanor García— whose very name grated on my father's nerves—was shouting, and over and over again above the din of the sirens we could hear him, already no more than three hundred meters away from the pier: *Uno, dos... Uno, dos... Uno, dos...*

García bent over the oar at the stern and pushed with all his might: *Uno, dos...*

At that moment I heard my father's calm, strong voice. Standing erect, steering oar grasped firmly, as if it were nailed to the spot, he commanded: *Jedan, dva...Jedan, dva... Jedan, dva...*

And the white boat left the red one behind, sliding by it "slippery as a fish" and at an incredible speed.

Rowing with long, sweeping strokes, but giving it their all, the twelve men seemed riveted to their benches; their bulging arm muscles, under their blue jerseys, about to explode. A tremendous shout rose from the pier. People applauded. Swift as the wind the white boat crossed the finish line, and immediately twelve oars were lifted vertically out of the water in perfect alignment. The jubilant shout of victory resounded: "Ra, ra, ra,... Chile and Dalmatia!"

Once more my father maneuvered with the steering oar and the boat slowly approached the pier. One crew member tied up the boat and the entire team, oars in hand, dexterously climbed the narrow stairs. They lined up single file, just as I had seen them rehearse, sweaty, gaze fixed, chests stuck out, hands at shoulder height holding their oars, while my father reported to the judge of the competition. The judge, an officer with stripes almost down to his elbows, saluted my father in military fashion. My father clicked his heels energetically and announced, "Maritime Society of Punta Arenas."

The high official, followed by an aide and accompanied by my father, went over to the winning team. Out of a red velvet box held by the aide, he took gold medals with tricolored ribbons and pinned them to the chest of each crew member. Finally, amid the thronging spectators, he turned to my father, decorated him with a larger medal, and embraced him.

The regimental band—which I hadn't noticed until then, so engrossed was I in all that was happening—broke into a lively tune, and once again the sirens on the boats blasted away. That Sunday afternoon, for the first time in my life, I shed tears of happiness. My younger brothers clapped and jumped for joy. Tío Juan smiled blissfully, and Lucho, trying to light a cigarette with shaking hands, murmured: "Darn the old man! Darn him! Now I know whom to take after!"

Barba Jule, Kum Jakov, Kum Grgo... all of them were there. Kum Ivon blew his nose resoundingly into a red handkerchief and kept repeating: "Chile and Dalmatia... Chile and Dalmatia... Chile and Dal...!"

There was a big celebration. It began at our house. I don't know how Mama managed to prepare such an excellent meal for the whole crew and the ten or twelve close friends who also showed up. The inventory of the Tres Estrellas practically disappeared as can after can of preserves was opened. The barrels of white and red wine were about to run dry. All guests were in high spirits. Someone had brought an accordion. Ancient Slavic songs resounded throughout the neighborhood. Even the soldiers on guard that Sunday afternoon got their share of broiled chicken and sweets, which my father, still wearing his gold medal, surreptitiously took to them.

It was almost dusk when the victors and the rest of the assembled guests decided to go first to the Maritime Society, then on to the Dalmatian Club.[42] Only

---

[42] Since 1915 this club co-existed with the "Croatian Club." In 1918 the "Croatian Club" changed its name to "Yugoslav Club," while the "Dalmatian Club" kept its identity. The "Dalmatian Society" exists to this day. The same is true of the "Yugoslav Club" which, however, reverted to its former name "Croatian Club" in 1991, after the outbreak of the Balkan War.

we children stayed behind to help our mother with the dishes. The fat Rosalía, no doubt exhausted by all the chores (and possibly from having taken more than one hurried swig when she went to refill the bottles in the cellar), had fallen asleep, resting her head on one corner of the table. Mama, tired but contented, and understanding as always, remarked: "One doesn't win a gold medal every day!"

It seemed to me that her voice, for the first time, betrayed a trace of pride. I looked at her, surprised. At that, she put her hand on my head and, speaking slowly, almost sadly, said: "When you get to be a sailor, my son, you'll also bring me gold medals and many beautiful things from all over the globe. But all I want is a rosary made out of olive pits from the Garden of Gethsemane."

I cried for the second time that day.

Happiness swept over me. I dreamed of marvelous, far-off worlds. My hands hurt from gripping the steering wheel of my boat of fantasies for so long.

I told my classmates I'd be a sailor.

"You're a bit skinny," one of them observed.

"I'll put on weight later," I told him. "Haven't you noticed my father? He weighs 120 kilos. He can knock off your papa's head with one single punch."

***

Yes, it was an eventful year. Among other occurrences, the statue of Ferdinand Magellan was unveiled. Papa told us that none other than the King of Spain's brother had come to the ceremony. As a result, the local Spaniards were bursting with pride. Many ambassadors, ministers, and other very important personages had traveled to Punta Arenas, which never before had received such a multitude of illustrious visitors and would probably never see such distinguished guests again. The sum squandered on just one day of these lavish festivities could no doubt have kept our family fed and clothed for a whole year.

The monument was beautiful and impressive. High above the ground loomed Don Ferdinand, scanning the horizon from the bow of his vessel, one foot on the bowsprit. To the sides of the pedestal, two Indians, one from Tierra del Fuego and one from Patagonia, represented the two shores of the Strait; the background depicted some complicated symbols referring to the circumnavigation of the world. There were also some bas-reliefs showing the ships in their struggle against uncharted seas and, of course, a plaque in large letters displaying the name of the statue's donor: José Menéndez. This plaque caused some tongue wagging at first. The monument was so grandiose, however, that people simply conceded that Don José was a very rich man without whose money there would have been no statue. At least that's how my father reasoned, as we kept walking around the wide pedestal examining every detail. According to Papa, the best thing about it all was that the monument was destined to honor a great sailor.

Actually, I was much more fascinated by the strange and beautiful flags decorating the square that afternoon, and by the brilliantly lit mansions surrounding it. Casa España, the elegant and proud center of the activities of the large Hispanic colony, had garlands of light and color adorning doors and windows. The mansions of Doña Sara Braun, Don José Menéndez, and Don Mauricio Braun, the impressive commercial establishment of Menéndez Behety and that of Braun and Blanchard, the Governor's Palace—all were brightly lit up from early evening on. Fireworks began as soon as it got dark. High above, on top of the hill, two sharp yellow traces delineated the cross against the night sky.

I felt a bit chilly but said nothing. There was so much more to see. Cars with mirrorlike windows framed by little silk curtains pulled up in front of Don José's mansion. From them emerged ladies with large hats, fur coats draped over sumptuous gowns, and gentlemen in top hats and evening clothes. A doorman in a braided uniform hurried to open car doors, doffing his cap ceremoniously. There also were officers in flashy uniforms with plumed helmets, red, golden or blue sashes, capes of various colors, and shiny sabers that clanged against even shinier boots, reflecting beams of light.

My father looked on in silence and twisted his mustache. His boots, too, had been polished to a high gloss. His coat was neatly buttoned; his hat sat very straight in military fashion. People were milling around. Many of our acquaintances passed by and we exchanged friendly greetings. The small and wiry Don Pablo Drpić, elegantly twirling his thin cane, came up to us, smiling: "Even if they erect twenty monuments like this one, they won't be able to beat us in a regatta, eh?"

My father laughed at the comment, but right away became serious: "They might defeat us at boccie ball. I've been watching them for weeks," he confided. "That Nicanor García and his buddies are going to cause us trouble."

Don Pablo became alarmed, and after a long silence, he announced: "They're going to challenge us to a bike race. We have Kragujić and Pesutić, but they have Vicente and Fernández and at least half a dozen more guys who don't do anything except ride around on their bikes all day. And do you know something else? They are getting a soccer team together."

"I don't like soccer. To kick a ball around is fine for kids, but for grown-ups... frankly I think it's plain stupid."

"But we'll still have to get up a team."

"Sure! And we'll put in the 'Turk,' Kalazić, so he can break their shins."

Don Pablo roared with laughter: Nikola Kalazić was a giant of a man. If he struck a table with his fist, he could cave it in as if it were a shoebox. Besides, he was tough in every sense of the word.

Don Pablo traced a few flourishes in the air with his cane and doffed his hat again and again whenever a group of people went by. He knew everybody and everybody knew him. He was the eternal Don Juan, never failing to tip his hat to a lady.

My father gave a half smile, pulling at his mustache.

"D'you know, Don Pablo? We've got to get up a good team of sharpshooters. We have the people for that: Marko Radojković, and some of the new guys. Yes, we have more than enough people for that."

"What about you?"

"Yes, I'd join."

"You'll have to be captain."

"No way, Don Pablo. I am Patron of the Boats and that's plenty. I believe in dividing responsibilities. When we start the soccer club one day soon, let the ablest player be captain. The boccie ball team should be headed up by Frane, in spite of his ugly temper. He's a good ball player. Sure, he insulted you, but he learned his lesson."

"As to bike racing, Jakov Pesutić should be asked to take that on; he knows all about biking. Everyone in his specialty, though if need be, we'll all pull together."

In the kiosk the band played taps, as we took one last leisurely turn around the square, greeting acquaintances every few steps. Papa and Don Pablo were in high spirits.

At one corner of the square stood the *barquillero*, an amusing Spaniard, in a spotlessly white shirt. He carried his *barquillos*[43] in a large drum-shaped container, a homemade roulette wheel fastened to its lid.

"Give it a try, boy!"

A two-cent coin bought a customer the right to spin the wheel. The number you landed on entitled you to that many *barquillos*. Depending on your luck, the wheel might stop on any number from one to twelve, but the twelve came up very rarely. The three came up most frequently. For me the wheel stopped at seven. "You ruined me," joked the vendor.

My father gave him another copper coin and spun the wheel himself: The one came up. "We're even," said my father.

***

Tío Juan didn't get up the next morning. When we came home at noon, he was still in bed, and Mama took

---

[43] Crunchy, cylindrical pastries.

him some chicken broth and a cup of herbal tea made from linden blossoms. This infusion had been recommended by Doña Marietta Kuščić who attended all the sick from our neighborhood on the hill, and—as I was to learn later—many from very distant barrios as well. Be that as it may, the "weeds," as Lucho called them, didn't help our uncle, and by afternoon his fever was so high that my father went to fetch the doctor.

Dr. Béncur came in quietly. He wore a wide-brimmed hat, a thick, light-colored raincoat, heavy boots, and, wrapped around his neck, a wool scarf. He carried a sturdy cane. His short, pointed beard was carefully trimmed. I thought he looked exactly as a physician should look.

Lucho commented under his breath: "You'll see: the old goat will give him an enema."

The doctor spent a long time with our uncle. Then he stuck his head out the door and called my father; both disappeared into Tío Juan's room. We waited a long while; the silence became oppressive. Mama moved her lips in a whisper. After an eternity we heard footsteps along the hallway.

Pneumonia was Dr. Béncur's verdict. Mama right away ordered us to stay out of Tío Juan's room until he was strong enough to get out of bed. The doctor wrote out the prescription on one corner of the dining table but waved Papa's five pesos aside. "No need. I'll bill you when the patient has improved. I'll be back tomorrow."

He bowed to my mother, took his hat and cane and left, accompanied by my father, who went to the *botica*.[44]

Lucho, now quite impressed by the kindly physician, exclaimed: "Damn, he's exactly like the doctor in your reader, exactly like him!"

Lucho didn't know that all the children of our family, for one reason or another, owed their life to Dr. Mateo Béncur. He had seen us through scarlet fever and whooping cough and had gone from our house to many, many others, close by or far away, poor or well-to-do, climbing steep streets full of frozen puddles or gooey mud, braving fierce winter nights, struggling against wind, rain, or snow at any time, any day. And many, many times, instead of writing out a prescription, he had dug from the big pockets of his raincoat the pills or the little flask that was needed, claiming that he just happened to have an extra bottle of the stuff; so there was no point in wasting money and making the *boticario* rich. And having said that, he would smile roguishly, give the little patient an affectionate pat, and take off, promising to be back the

---

[44] Store that sells medications prepared by a pharmacist (*boticario*) as well as prepacked pharmaceutical remedies and all kinds of health-related products.

next day—but only if it were necessary. He had to make too many calls to care about small bills.

Dr. Béncur was not Dalmatian. Some said he was Hungarian; others alleged he was Czech or Polish, or even Russian. But he spoke like a Dalmatian and considered himself to be one. More than once he sat down with our family to share our simple, workday lunch. Only on such occasions would he take off his raincoat, drink a glass of wine, and smoke a cigarette while having a long chat with my father. Both men liked to reminisce about Vienna. My father had been there only once, when, as a seaman first class on the Austro-Hungarian navy school ship Saida, he marched in a parade past Emperor Francis Joseph. The doctor, at the time a student in the Austrian capital, happened to watch that very parade. Memories of the event linked the two men.

In a few days Tío Juan was out of danger. Though pale and weak, he joined us in the kitchen and sat down on the woodbox. There were shadows under his eyes; his expression was even sadder than usual.

We heard the doorbell of the grocery store. The Italian mailman Mattioni announced in a clear voice: "Lettera... a letter from Europe!"

The letter was for Tío Juan. He opened the envelope nervously and, before unfolding the page, kept turning it around and around until Mama demanded: "Read it, Juan!"

Tío Juan read in silence; his eyes filled with tears, but they were tears of happiness. His distant beloved had said yes.

The next day, still pale and still a bit shaky, our uncle, accompanied by my father, bought a return passage to Dalmatia, to Brač, to Pučišće, to his homeland ("Tamo daleko, daleko kraj mora...")

***

I was in for a special treat. Papa let me go along in the motor launch that took Tío Juan out to the great steamer flying the British flag.

Clutching my father's hand so hard my fingers hurt, I stood next to him on the small deck of the prow, inhaling the pungent sea air and holding on to my sailor hat with my free hand. As soon as the launch brushed against the steamer's companionway, my father scooped me up in his arms and leaped onto the steps. He took the wobbly steps two at a time. My uncle followed behind with difficulty, hindered by his limp and his suitcases. For the first time in my life I found myself on board a real ocean liner.

The third-class passengers were quartered in the stern. We climbed down iron ladders and made our way along narrow, dark corridors. The cabin was big; it had ten or twelve bunks. Many other people arrived at the same time we did, carrying bundles, suitcases, trunks, and duffle bags. There was barely any space to move.

My father pointed to a top bunk in a corner near a porthole and told my uncle: "That's the best one. Throw your luggage up there. Here, as everywhere else, the early bird catches the worm." And he helped him stash away his bags. "You'll be fine here. Soon you'll have made friends with everybody, and the voyage will be over before you know it."

A nervous, lively Italian was looking for a berth for himself. My father took him by the arm: "Gaetano, this is my brother-in-law Juan. You'll be traveling together. Take the bunk right under his. It's the best one. You're going to have a good time. I wish I could go with you."

Gaetano stretched out his hand, and my uncle shook it warmly. It was no small matter that my father's simple diplomacy had procured him a companion with whom to exchange a few words... that is, if the Italian would ever stop talking.

"I've been here for ten years and I barely earned enough to get by. *Madonna Santa!* And all this time my wife's been sleeping alone in Napoli," he spluttered in a mixture of broken Italian and Spanish.

The four of us were sitting on Gaetano's bunk for quite a while; I had fun, watching my father and my uncle shake with suppressed laughter, as the Neapolitan kept running his mouth... Suddenly a bell rang.

"We've got to leave, son," said my father. "Say goodbye to your uncle."

Tío Juan hugged me tightly and kissed me on my forehead, right on the spot under the place where it said "Esmeralda"[45] on the ribbon of my sailor hat. I began to pick my way through the mounds of luggage and the people crowding the cabin. Looking back I saw my father, standing on a trunk, take out his wallet and hand several bills up to my uncle. "It's a long trip," I heard him say. "You'll need some gold to buy something special to eat or when the ship puts into port. If something's left over, use it to get a present for your fiancée. Goodbye, Juan!"

They shook hands for a long, long time, not saying a word.

I climbed down the companionway from the liner by myself and took Papa's hand only when I had to jump back into the launch. The sea was white-capped now, and the wind sprayed us with salty droplets. The great ship blasted its siren—a deep and prolonged sound that seemed like another handshake. The passengers were leaning on the railing. We waved our handkerchiefs as the launch shoved off. At every hoot of the siren, we noticed a thin column of white smoke rising next to the steamer's chimney, like another handkerchief fluttering in the afternoon.

From the pier we watched the liner recede into the distance until we could no longer make out the people on

---

[45] Name of the Chilean Navy School Ship.

board. Papa lit a cigar and began to stride inland. I kept up with him. "You're a big boy now. No need to take my hand."

I felt proud. Maybe I could really be a sailor.

***

Mama was sad; Papa was silent. Something seemed to be missing in the house. Maybe it was my uncle's uneven step. Or his heartfelt songs. Lucho kept to himself and went out for extended periods, getting home later every night. Finally my father decided to put a stop to that.

One evening, when we were all sitting around the table, he said calmly, weighing his words very carefully: "Not everybody can leave; nor can everybody stay. A man needs more than food and sleep. Juan left, because his place is over there. That's where he has everything he loves. There he understands the Gospels, because they are read in his language... Nothing is gained by refusing to acknowledge reality... We, on the other hand, we belong here. That, too, is a reality. What do you say Lucho?"

"I'm neither from here nor from there."

"Why's that?"

"Because I left there as a small child. I roamed the pampa for ten years. I was a boy and became a man, surrounded by herds of wild horses, Tehuelche Indians, *pacos*,[46] 'Turks,' gringos, and Gallegos.[47] I broke in horses; I hung out in low dives; I defended myself at gunpoint from bandits... I don't have a homeland... For some I was "the kid," for others the "the little Austrian" or "the little gringo." In my mind I was an abandoned child... who only recently got to meet his old man."

My father's steely glance softened: "You're right, my son. It's true. But now you *are* at home, and these are your brothers and this is your mother..."

"Yes; I love her a lot, but she's not my mother, although she's so very, very kind. Damn! Makes me feel like crying." And he got up brusquely and locked himself in his room.

My father got up too and went to the store. There he sat down on his heavy wooden chair and unfolded the newspaper.

Mama made us go to bed early. A violent wind howled outside.

The next day was clear and cold. The first snow brought enchantment to the streets. On our way to school we hurled big snowballs and had fun making footprints in the white expanse where no one had walked before us.

In the schoolyard the bigger boys built more or less grotesque white statues. We named them after some

---

[46] In Chile, pejorative for policemen.
[47] Natives of Galicia, a region in the northeast of Spain.

of our teachers, and called one "Guatón,"[48] the nickname of our rotund playmate Barria. Sadly, by eleven, the sun had reduced all this artistry to water and mud.

Sloshing around in the puddles, we returned home, our shoes filled with icy water, our stockings soaked. We were shivering, sneezing, and blowing our noses stentoriously. We had caught tremendous colds. Mama put us to bed with hot water bottles and made us drink milk with honey, which, fortunately, wasn't bad.

By contrast, the cod-liver oil ordered by Dr. Béncur was most unpleasant. We were to take one spoonful before each meal. How disgusting!! We tried everything. We claimed the spoon was too big, that "the stuff" smelled horrid... But nothing worked. The military discipline with which our house was run brooked no excuses. So we had to down that repulsive liquid. It saved our lives to be sure, but at what a cost!

---

[48] Chilean idiom for "potbelly."

4

TEN YEARS AS AN ORPHAN

"Damn! I've been through so much I can hardly remember all of it." Lucho put his guitar down on his bed, lit a cigarette, and got ready to tell us about his life. It was Sunday, shortly after lunch. Outside, snow was falling gently; the stillness was profound. The snow stuck to roofs and fence poles and electrical cables; the telephone wires looked immensely thick. Ever so often you could hear the crunching footsteps of someone walking past on the street.

It was dark before Lucho finished his story, a long and strange account in which the bitterness of solitude was intertwined with the lighthearted cheerfulness of youth. Perhaps Lucho's tranquil gaze and easygoing smile stemmed from all of these experiences, lived through so serenely and so naturally. Coming and going among the flock of his memories, he at times fell silent, absorbed by some distant event he might have preferred to forget. At such an instant he took a deep breath, lit another cigarette, managed a smile—which put fine wrinkles on his face—and resumed his tale.

His father had left for the Americas before he was born. This was a period of emigration that would last several years and during which the men went off alone, with the idea of returning to fetch their families or sending for them. In Lucho's case, as in that of so many others, the separation that was supposed to last merely a few months lasted almost ten years. And in many instances the wives never heard from their husbands again. America was in a part of the world from which very few returned and from which news took months to arrive.

When Lucho's father was at last able to send the money for the tickets, the boy and his mother were counting on meeting him in the Argentinian Patagonia. But a whole year went by before mother and son could procure the necessary documents and put together the things they needed for the voyage. By the time they finally arrived at the designated spot, Lucho's father, enticed by new prospects of making a fortune, had left with a group of his countrymen for the Bolivian highlands and, from there, to who knows where!

Some Dalmatian compatriots who had already been in Patagonia for many years helped the woman find work and made sure that the boy went to school for a while to learn Spanish.

"But not a sign from the old man," said Lucho, scratching himself behind one ear. "I had come to meet him, but damn! Now I would have to find him first."

With this idea fixed in his mind, Lucho, then barely eleven years old, without knowing anything about anything, imagining all of the Americas to be no bigger than his native island of Brać, without a cent in his pocket, left home one evening and got on a train. The train went inland; Lucho had seen gauchos and foreigners ride it.

That night Lucho's adventures began. They were to last more than a decade.

The train was headed nowhere, because the tracks to the settlement of Las Heras, which was to be the boy's destination, had not yet been completed. Along with the crowd of motley passengers the boy reached one of the two hotels of the village. There, in exchange for washing dishes, he received room and board and, in addition, fifteen pesos a month.

Many people stopped at the hotel: long-maned gauchos, their *facón*[49] stuck in their *faja*,[50] "Turkish" peddlers, traveling to the "interior" in search of Tehuelche tent camps; police officers in pursuit of cattle thieves and bandits; an occasional missionary priest; heavily made-

---

[49] Large knife with a single blade, used for fighting but also for slaughtering and skinning cattle.
[50] Black woven sash gauchos often wear instead of a leather belt.

up, gaudily dressed women who laughed loudly and drank gin—in short, all types.

"My *patrón*,[51] a Spaniard, as kind-hearted as they come, though given to spouting terrible invectives and blasphemies, noticing that I was itching to take off after the peddlers, the cattle thieves, and the women, gave me some sound advice; but I felt I couldn't stay put."

Early one Monday morning, after the departure of all the clients who came on Sundays to win or lose fortunes playing *truco*[52] and *taba*,[53] Lucho saddled an old nag "to take a little canter" around the hills. This was his favorite and only pastime to relieve the week's drudgery.

Relaxed, without a worry, he randomly spurred on his horse, but on the whole let it run freely, when he noticed a group of ostriches raising their inquiring heads on long skinny necks. Following his first enthusiastic impulse and without realizing the uselessness of his attempt, Lucho dug in his spurs and gave chase. But an ostrich first runs in a straight line and then, when it seems about to be caught, abruptly changes direction, repeating this game over and over. There's not a horse alive that

---

[51] Boss

[52] Card game originally from Southern France and Catalonia, played with a standard Spanish forty-card deck.

[53] A betting game of Greek origin, introduced in Argentina and Chile by the Spaniards, in which a bone from an animal's foot is tossed in a court traced on the ground by lines a few meters apart. If the bone falls with the concave side up, the player wins; if it falls with the flat side facing up, he loses.

can keep this up. Besides, every ostrich in the group takes off in a different direction!

The result was that Lucho, galloping in wild spurts, wound up so far from the hotel that darkness overtook him. There he was in the middle of the pampa, disoriented and alone on the back of a worn-out and trembling jade.

Ambling haphazardly up a hill, he discerned a feeble light in the distance and headed toward it. Half an hour later he dismounted at the hitching rack of an estancia[54] that he recognized as the one belonging to the Basques some four leagues from the village. He knew that in these solitary places, where banditry was rampant, people took justice in their own hands and there wasn't anyone without a trusty Colt stuck in his belt. For this reason he couldn't just go up to the door and knock; that might get him shot. So, from a distance, he let out the shout used by all friends: "Ave Maríaaaaaa!"

What started as shelter for one night turned into months of cheerful and pleasant fellowship; and even though his *patrón* came to look for him, Lucho preferred staying at the estancia "to learn how to work and later on to take a quick look at the world."

One Sunday an "Austrian" arrived from Santa Cruz. He had been searching for Lucho for two months in

---

[54] Large cattle ranch.

village after village, estancia after estancia. He brought bad news for him: his mother had died.

The Basques solemnly gathered around, turning and turning their berets in their hands, looking at that terribly surprised kid. At last the foreman, Don Ignacio, crossed himself and whispered: "May she rest in peace. Amen."

***

Lucho walked up to the window and, looking at the snow, which kept falling gently, said hoarsely: "At that moment I really felt alone; but damn! Also freer than ever!"

The reminiscence caused him to remain silent for a while. He ground out his cigarette stub against the heel of his shoe and seemed to be looking for a way to shorten his narration.

***

Hardened by backbreaking work, violent storms in summer, treacherous snowfalls, and deadly icy blasts in winter, risking his life in every rodeo, on each journey, and even during each spree, the boy slowly became a man. He was tall, strong, agile, sharp-eyed, and dexterous, firm on the back of the fiercest mount, swift with the lasso and *boleadoras*,[55] but also able to strum a

---

[55] Weapon or tool that the gaucho*s* copied from the Indians. A two- or three-thonged lasso with a ball of stone, iron, wood, or lead, covered

guitar and sing a romantic ditty by a window discreetly left half open.

One day Don Ignacio asked whether Lucho had an ample supply of bullets for his Colt, a good *facón*, a sharp knife, and an accurate long-range rifle. Lucho had all of those things and, in addition, owned two good horses, lassos of guanaco hide, and several pairs of *boleadoras*. "In that case we'll ride inland."

That's what Lucho wanted: to ride inland, to the unknown "interior" of the pampa, beyond the Tehuelche camps, where there was nothing but open space and untamed, wild animals.

They took off one Sunday at dawn, two handsome gauchos, *chambergos*[56] cocked, ponchos, *bombachas*,[57] soft leather boots, silk kerchiefs around their neck, big-wheeled spurs, silver-studded harnesses and saddles, *facones* stuck into wide belts with interior pockets and large buckles, good rifles and 44s peeping out from under their coats.

A couple of months' labor could mean returning with a drove of thirty or forty well-tamed horses. But it was extremely hard work. The two men by themselves had to catch, break in, and brand the animals—all in the

---

by untanned leather, attached to the end of each thong. Used to catch ostriches, deer, horses and cattle; by entangling their feet.
[56] Hats with turned-up brims worn by gauchos.
[57] Baggy gaucho trousers either stuffed into short boots (as was the case here) or worn with *alpargatas*, rope-soled canvas shoes.

open pampa—always keeping one eye on their task and one on the horizon, whence Indians or bandits might appear at any moment.

Nonetheless, the job got done, and done well. Don Ignacio was pleased, and, in high spirits, they started on the road back. After they had ridden for many days, the low ridges of the estancia rose in the distance. The foreman stopped his horse: "So what do you say Lucho? We made it back!"

"That's true for you, Don Ignacio. I'll take my leave here. I'm returning to the wilds. I'm curious to get to where the Indians live."

Arguments, entreaties, curses, and blasphemies, both in Basque and Spanish, couldn't convince Lucho to remain at the estancia. Unmoved by Don Ignacio's despair, Lucho and his little drove soon were nothing but a small cloud of dust in the distance.

***

The Tehuelches lived quite well. They were the undisputed masters of the land. No alien authority or laws constrained them. They devoted themselves to amassing herds of cattle and preparing guanaco or mare *charqui*.[58] And even in this task they were easy-going. They hunted only *chulenguitos*, ignoring the full-grown guanacos because they were more difficult to catch. In their tents—

---

[58] Jerky.

large as houses and constructed from very sturdy and tightly lashed branches covered by forty or fifty guanaco skins—lived entire families, from the grandfather on down. The chief of the tribe wielded power as limitless as the pampa. Neither he nor his sons knew how to count the many heads of cattle they owned.

Distrustful at first, they soon came to like the tanned, blue-eyed youth who was able to perform the most demanding jobs.

There was no shortage of *yerba mate*, savory *asados*,[59] and an occasional drink of gin, the latter obtained through barter from the adventurers passing through when they happened to be in need of a horse. The visits of these foreigners left other imprints as well: very pretty half-breed women, almost white, eyes bright as water.

Lucho stayed with the Tehuelches for three months, working little and having the Indian girls teach him their language in the shelter of some thicket or some large rock that protected as much from the wind as from curious onlookers. A young Indian widow who owned more heads of cattle than the Basques at their estancia asked Lucho to marry her—a rather tempting proposal for more reasons than one. Lucho already had visions of

---

[59] Roasts on the spit.

himself as a rancher, surrounded by little mestizo children.

But then the cold weather set in; it was no longer possible to sleep under the open sky. At first one, then two guanaco blankets barely sufficed to get warm. And that's when Lucho's sufferings began. Terrible itching kept him awake all night, tossing and turning on his camp bed. Lice, also in search of warmth, became a real scourge. It was useless to shake out the blankets before making up the bed: the bothersome vermin seemed to come out of the walls, from the floor, from everywhere.

In the end the lice proved stronger than love, and one fine day, accompanied by his dogs, Lucho and his herd took off at a lively trot, heading south.

The following summer he worked with the *tropas*[60] or caravans of carts and lorries that transported goods from the estancias to the railroad. Each *tropa* consisted of ten or more carts pulled by mules or by four, five, and even six teams of oxen and some huge wagons with enormous wheels, each pulled by twenty-four horses. Amid the dust and the wind, the only person who rode in comfort was the leader of the column; the others moved in a dense cloud of dust, chewing dirt. The slow round trip took an entire day. The men spent the night sleeping in the now empty carts right in the courtyard of the station;

---

[60] Literally, "troop."

they returned the following day in the same vehicles, getting their kidneys pounded, as sparks flew from the animals' hooves knocking against the rocks. A season's pay yielded heavy silver pesos, but they were quickly spent on card games, bets, and wild sprees.

Lucho soon found it boring to keep riding along the same paths, "because it cannot be one's destiny to be harnessed to some wagon like a mule."

So once more he trotted off across the expanse of the pampa without a definite goal, his herd in front, followed by his dogs and his packhorse. Any thicket would do as his shelter for the night, and when, at daybreak, the sun steeped the *coirones*[61] in gold, Lucho was up brewing *mate* and grilling a *churrasco*.[62] In this manner, riding from estancia to estancia, from small farm to small farm, and hiring himself out for a day or for several months, time went by.

***

Lucho had turned eighteen, or maybe nineteen. He had just finished delivering a small herd he had been commissioned to break in and his belt was stuffed with bills. Along the way he came across the tents of some "Turkish" peddlers and used the opportunity to buy clothes, new boots, and a good poncho, as well as a few

---

[61] Tall grass, fodder for the animals inhabiting the pampas, also used as material in the construction of modest houses.
[62] Steak.

silk kerchiefs in case he wanted to stop at some settlement; he also acquired two bottles of gin. Feeling like taking a few days' rest, he decided to visit José Cares, a Spaniard who owned a small estancia and who could always use the help of friends.

There Lucho whiled away his time, half idly, dipping sheep, riding overland, breaking in some *redomón*,[63] and drinking *mate* by the open fire. But one day at dawn, he and Don José were woken by the sound of hooves; half-dressed, they ran to the door, rifles in hand. At the hitching rack of the house, wrapped in a dust cloud tinged gold by the morning sun, they saw a large contingent of strange-looking horsemen. The tips of their helmets, their rifles slung across their chests, their long sabers hanging from their mounts, and the buttons of their tunics—all were glistening. There were many of them: a few fair and robust, with braids, laurels, and gold stars; the others dark-skinned, thin and virtually floating inside their uniforms. And behind them was a variegated bunch of unarmed peasants, guarded by half a dozen blond giants cantering around them in circles as if they were herding cattle.

Even before the officer in charge stated his business, Don José and Lucho realized that they were looking at a detachment of the Frontier Squadron,

---

[63] Hard-to-train bronco.

charged with establishing law and order in Patagonia and organized by German instructors, veterans of the War of 1914.

Shortly after their arrival, one of the Germans, assisted by a *criollo* adjutant, filled out a form with information provided by the elderly Don José, who was trembling with fear. The officer found everything to be in order except for Lucho's presence. According to the German, no one had any business paying visits and working for free. Without much ceremony Lucho was stuck in the line of unarmed peasants, though not without requesting and receiving a statement acknowledging the confiscation of his revolver, his rifle, his dagger, and four hundred *pesos nacionales.*

The detachment camped out for five days at Don José's estancia without much to keep them occupied. The German officers and sergeants tried to teach the dark-skinned recruits—most of them northerners from the provinces of Córdoba and Catamarca, and most of them mulattos—how to handle weapons and ride horses like soldiers and not like Indians; the prisoners were put to work skinning animals, feeding the horses, and performing a few other chores, but parceled out among so many, these tasks barely kept them busy for a few hours. In consequence, the prisoners spent most of their time drinking *mate*, smoking, chatting, and, above all, trying to figure out a way to escape. The latter proved to be simply impossible. As soon as it got dark, the Germans tied the prisoners up in pairs, shackling right wrist to right wrist or left to left, thus preventing any coordinated movement on their part.

Sometimes, during the day, Don José managed to get one of the sergeants to allow Lucho to help him with his work, but when Lucho did so, he was followed by a German with a gun ready to shoot.

In the end, everybody got to know everyone else, the prisoners as well as the *milicos*.[64] Four officers ate and slept in Don José's house; three sergeants, five corporals, and some forty privates—most of them part Indian, looking like cutthroats—camped out. In addition, there was a young boy who played the drum and polished the commander's boots.

There were horses galore: two mounts for every soldier and two dozen mules to pull the two heavy *chatas*[65] that transported the two small cannons, munitions, tents, supplies, uniforms—in short, everything needed by a detachment on campaign. Furthermore, there were forty-three detainees who owned more than two hundred horses between them.

Discipline was harsh. Anyone stepping outside the camp by even a millimeter would risk getting shot. The boss of all these forces, sometimes on horseback

---

[64] In Spanish, rather pejorative term for "military."
[65] Flat wagons, lorries.

but almost always on foot and accompanied by his adjutant, would regularly inspect the orderly array of tents and campfires. He was a German major, ruddy, stout, and stern-faced, with a stomping walk.

One morning at about ten o'clock a corporal came looking for Lucho to take him to the commander. Seated at the table of Don José's modest house, which had been converted into general headquarters, wearing his helmet and looking stiffer than ever, the major stated his terms without any circumlocutions: "You are a scout for this region. I offer you 150 pesos per month and the grade of sergeant to lead us—by the shortest route possible—to Río Gallegos. Do you accept?"

For a moment Lucho stood dumbfounded; but then, out of the corner of his eye, he caught Don José's worried expression, making signs to him that he should agree.

"I accept. We'll get there in twenty days, sir."

"Very well. Select a patrol from among the soldiers."

The only part of the uniform Lucho would wear was the coat with the wide golden epaulettes. He hung his saber next to his lasso and put the gun assigned to him among the gear carried by his packhorse. He felt better and more secure with his Colt and his *carabine*, his *facón*, and his *boleadoras*. He wanted nothing to do with the recruits and demanded to be permitted to choose his five-men patrol from among the prisoners. The commander had to agree; he knew full well that neither his German veterans, nor his lazy recruits from up north would do him any good in these latitudes, this borderless expanse where you had to find your way by the stars, the wind, and the smells.

Before daybreak the large detachment took off in a southerly direction. Lucho rode at the head with his patrol. A bit farther back came the commander and his officers; still farther back the prisoners, then the soldiers, the lorries carrying the baggage, and, at the rear, the huge number of animals kept in check by a few gauchos, who in turn were guarded by eight soldiers, arms at the ready.

During the long days of the forced march the squadron was engaged in "cleansing operations." They crammed the jails of all the settlements they passed through with suspects. Cattle thieves and bandits caught red-handed were dispatched by four bullets in the chest; their bodies remained behind as macabre markers along the route of the detachment across the pampa. The German commander carried the law in his cartridge belt and applied it summarily and coldly.

One evening when they were dismounting to pitch camp next to a little stream, Lucho went up to the commander: "Sir, if we make an early start tomorrow, we can be in Río Gallegos by lunchtime. It's over there, a little to the left, behind that blue hill in the distance. Can't you smell the ocean air?"

And the next day, around noon, greeted by a military band, flags, and applause, the odd detachment entered the small capital of the Territory of Santa Cruz. Lucho rode bewildered among the noncommissioned officers, for the first time wearing the complete uniform and a helmet that was too small for him.

That same afternoon, while the others were cleaning their uniforms in the courtyard of the barracks, Lucho went to return his to the officer on duty. Some difficulties arose. The officer did not feel authorized to permit Lucho to leave. But providentially, the commander appeared at this juncture and said, "Lucho, you kept your promise. You brought us this far. You are free to go."

And he proffered his hand, cordially and energetically. Lucho signed a paper, received his pay of 150 pesos, and went into the street armed with his *facón* and his revolver. He would come back later for the rest of his money, his rifle, and his horses.

But things got complicated. The Argentine government wanted to clean up Patagonia, and foreigners lacking a fixed occupation and the proper documents began to have a hard time. It didn't make any difference to have grown up in the pampa and to be as good a gaucho as any.

In town Lucho luckily ran into several "Austrians"—Buratović, Martinović, and Pivčević. The latter made the mail run to Punta Arenas in a Model T Ford. He told Lucho: "I know your father is in Punta Arenas. I'll take you. But who'll pay?" Pivčević was a good chap, although a bit too keen on money. Lucho offered him the 150 pesos from his sergeant's pay.

***

Silence fell. I looked at the window and noticed that the glass had turned black; outside the whiteness had gone out of the day. In the half-light Lucho struck a match, and while he was lighting another cigarette, some fine, almost imperceptible wrinkles marked the tension in his face, which was normally so cheerful. He looked at me as an equal, as one brother looks at another, and then he spoke with a slight tremor in his words, which came out hesitantly in spite of his effort not to attach importance to them: "I didn't need anybody to tell me he was my father. After all, we looked alike except for an age difference of thirty years. He stood in the middle of the hall of the Royal Hotel, well dressed, boots polished to a gloss, his coat buttoned all the way, his hat on straight. And there was I,—damn!—looking like a gaucho, my poncho around my shoulders, my short boots, and my Colt and my *facón* sticking out from beneath my jacket. He walked toward me slowly, biting his mustache, and I didn't budge, not knowing what to do. I put out my hand,

and wow! He threw himself on me and gave me a hug that almost suffocated me. *¡La gran siete!* Lord Almighty! Next he put his hands on my shoulders and peered into my eyes as if he wanted to see the innermost part of my soul! I felt tears coming, like that time when they told me my mother had died."

Lucho flattened the stub of his cigarette with his foot and, recovering all his self-possession, added with a smile: "Oh, well... after being an orphan for some ten years, here I am!"

5

DALMATIANS AND YUGOSLAVS

The Hungarian Andrés Kopeski was short, but strong like those oaks that have more roots than branches and grow on mountains lashed by hurricanes. His was a tragic yet entertaining story, which he never failed to relate—half laughing, half crying—whenever he had a few drinks too many. It was hard to understand him because he spoke with a nasal stutter, not to mention his idiosyncratic mix of bad Spanish, bad Croatian, and possibly good Hungarian. They called him "Andresko," because when he introduced himself, he spouted out his name explosively so as not to get tongue-tied, and people understood "Andresko Peski."

As a youngster he'd been in some war or other. He was wounded. He deserted. They caught him and were going to shoot him. Actually, they did shoot him, but luckily the soldier in charge of his execution was a bad shot; he merely grazed Andresko's left ear, the ear behind which he always wore a carnation. He got married, but after two weeks his wife took off with another man. So Andresko, who had something of a gypsy nature, hired himself out as a stoker on a freighter flying the Greek flag. He fell sick on board, and the captain had him hospitalized in Punta Arenas. There Father José Savarino, believing the Hungarian to be a Christian, administered the last rites to him. Andresko recovered, abjured his native Islamic faith and became a Roman Catholic. Ever since he was always the first in line to carry the statue of whichever saint was taken to the streets in a procession.

Andresko used to come by our house during the long summer evenings or on winter Sundays before going to mass. He would have one or two glasses of *rakija* with my father and talk a mile a minute in spite of his stutter and strange dialect.

One particular Sunday my father had invited him to lunch. The Hungarian felt obliged to show up with a huge package of fruit that must have cost him an arm and a leg: Spanish grapes, Chilean apples, Brazilian bananas, tropical mangoes and a huge coconut that was to make a lot of trouble.

Instead of thanking his guest, as my mother had already done, my father scolded him: "You're crazy, Andresko. You must have spent a fortune on all this fruit.

I feel like throwing the coconut at your head; that would be the best way to crack it! *Bogami!*"

The Hungarian, red as a tomato, stuttered: "Don't angry, my friend. Don't angry! I didn't bring it fo- fo- for you. I br- ought it fo- for the kids. They are my friends. I- I- I- don't have any chi- chi- children."

My father smoothed his mustache without knowing what to say. We took care of the grapes, the mangoes, the bananas, and some of the apples in no time. But the coconut was another matter. Lucho tried to pry it open with his *facón*. Then he tried cracking it against the floor. No luck. "You stubborn coconut! Blast you!"

My father suggested cutting it open with a saw. But Andresko objected. "No, fi- first we have to find the holes, so- so- so we ca- ca- can get out the juice."

And he kept turning over the coconut in search of those holes. Mama burst out laughing and before too long we were all roaring with laughter until poor Andresko, flustered and furious, threw open the window and hurled the coconut out into the patio.

We children rushed after it into the snow, ready for mischief. But before long, Zvonko, who was about five by then, picked up the coconut and looked it over carefully. All of a sudden he found a hole in that impenetrable shell and easily stuck one of his small fingers into it. We all trooped back into the kitchen. Yes, sir, the coconut had three small holes, and Zvonko had found them!

Greatly relieved, it was now Andresko's turn to laugh. My father ceremoniously handed him his heavy "paving" hammer. Andresko, ready for vengeance, unhurriedly took the tool and the coconut and went outside. With his feet he cleared the snow from a small area, placed the coconut on that bare patch and came down on it with a ferocious blow, sending pieces of coconut in all directions and even causing sparks to fly where the hammer hit the pavement.

This incident would be remembered in many cheerful conversations around the family dinner table.

That afternoon, after lingering over dessert longer than usual, Papa and the Hungarian went to the Dalmatian Club, and we stayed outside to build snowmen along the street. Lucho disappeared into the shack at the far end of the patio to work on a sled he was building for us.

It got dark very early and we went indoors to do our homework. Mama was busy setting out our clothes for the next day. It started snowing again. Silence surrounded us.

Papa returned in time for supper. He was serious and taciturn. No doubt some discussion at the club had displeased him. After Mama cleared the table, he checked our exercise books and, satisfied with our scholarship, smiled at us affectionately; then he lit up the last cigar of the day. We knew that meant bedtime for us. Moments later the sound of taps came from the regimental headquarters.

***

That winter there were masses of snow and a few bothersome thaws that filled the streets with mud. Some nights so much snow collected on our roof that we could hear the rafters creak. In the morning Papa and Lucho had to climb on top of the house to push the snow off with shovels and brooms.

There were a few days when we couldn't even make it to school, because the snow was as deep as we were tall. But those were precisely the days we had the most fun. All the kids of the barrio got together in the street and had enthusiastic snowball fights that almost always ended with the smaller kids in tears because a snowball had hit them on the ear or in the eye. There were snowmen in front of every house; We enjoyed watching the enormous sleds distributing beer in our neighborhood. They were pulled by three powerful horses whose collars were decorated with little bells that made our street resound with their cheerful tinkle. By the time coal and firewood started to become scarce and things began to look bad, however, the sun reappeared and, with it, Oyarzún's cart, carrying an enormous load of firewood; or a shaky steam-powered truck from the

Loreto Mine, weighted down by a pyramid of sacks filled with coal; or butcher Sieger's little Model T Ford truck; or baker Don Pedro's cart; or Don Luka, our greengrocer, with baskets of cabbages standing on a small sled he pulled himself.

My father didn't remain idle either. To keep his grocery store well stocked, he went downtown almost daily. Sometimes he rented a cart to bring back boxes and sacks of merchandise: cigarettes, crackers, rice, pasta, liqueurs, wine barrels, and thousands of other items. The regiment was growing and, with it, the clientele of the Almacén Tres Estrellas.

At night, after closing time, when the doors had been bolted and the books balanced, my mother kneaded bread dough while my father—using a good brandy, aromatic herbs, and burnt sugar—concocted the *rakija* which—in the depth of the night after taps had sounded—was to tune up the bodies of officers, noncoms, and an occasional enlisted man. And of course Oyarzún, with the precision of a Swiss watch, would put his stamp of approval on the delicious strong drink the following morning.

Winter, apart from its hardships, had pleasant aspects. Friends and relatives dropped in more often, and their visits tended to be more prolonged and animated. Kum Grgo, Kum Jakov, Barba Jule, and Kum Ivon came by frequently and stayed for hours, engaged in lively discussions about how to fix the world's problems, now and then punctuating their conversations with a sip.

One day Don Visko Damjanović came by our house. He was tall, erect, and outgoing, yet once in a while a bit self-important and even boastful. Kum Ivon and the kindly, cheerful, and shy Barba Jule were already there.

Don Visko was neither "kum" nor "barba." He was simply a fellow countryman and a friend of my father's from early childhood. They had both been on board the *Saida*, doing their four long years of military service together. Sitting around a bottle of wine warmed by the heat of the kitchen, they soon were engrossed in a subject which until then they had discreetly circumvented.

"Yes," said Don Visko. "We already have a Yugoslav Club. What we need to do now is to merge the two clubs, our club and the Dalmatian one."

"I don't see why," said my father, and he added with feigned innocence: "Can't one be Dalmatian and Yugoslav at the same time?"

"I don't think so. We're going to remain what we are in any case; but I believe it's more convenient to call ourselves Yugoslavs."

Kum Ivon blinked nervously. "I don't see the difference, Visko. We're Dalmatians, Croats, if you wish; we speak our own language; we worship our God. Only yesterday we were Austrians and Dalmatians; in the same way, we can be Yugoslavs and Dalmatians. Austrians or Yugoslavs—we'll remain Dalmatians... Who can change that?"

"Don't toy with words, Black Cat!" roared Damjanović.

Kum Ivon said haughtily: "When Dalmatia was a kingdom, the Serbs were still eating raw meat."

My father exhaled a thick puff of blue smoke: "I don't have a problem putting a photograph of the Serbian king next to one of Francis Joseph and Arturo Alessandri.[66] None of that will change my way of being, nor my language, nor my ideas. But do you, Visko Damjanović, think that we who came here ought to meddle in matters that only those who stayed 'over there' can fix? Look at this country. Here every five years they elect a king—they call him 'president,' and they have this advantage: if they don't care for him, they throw him out. Whereas over there... Now they are putting a Serb over us, one of those who drove an ox-cart and herded sheep, cows, and horses in the mountains. If you compare him with Emperor Francis Joseph... well! *Bogami!* There simply is no comparison! There's a great distance between Vienna and Belgrade. But Zagreb will always be Zagreb."

---

[66] Chilean president, 1920–1925, and again 1932–1938. The reference here is to his first mandate.

They kept arguing for hours. And of course they couldn't reach an agreement. I, on the other hand, got tired of filling up the wine jug again and again, at shorter and shorter intervals. When they left, the house was full of tobacco smoke.

I had to listen to these same arguments on many a subsequent occasion. Each of the men understood patriotism in his own way. My father and Kum Ivon could not be budged; firmly, but taking great care not to offend the others, they stood their ground.

"We seem to be dealing with the old question: 'What came first, the chicken or the egg?'" remarked Kum Ivon one afternoon. "We've been Croats since time immemorial, and if the long Austrian domination didn't change us, why should the Serb domination change us now? Egg or chicken, we existed before the Austrians and the Serbs, and just as we managed to live with the former, we'll live with the latter."

"Right you are, kume,"[67] said my father approvingly: "The Austrian domination lasted a very long time; let's see how long the Serbian rule will last. Having been called 'Austrian,' I could care less if they now call me 'Yugoslav.' The only thing I would mind is if one fine day they took it into their heads to call me 'Turk' or 'Italian.'"

---

[67] Vocative of *kum*

Nonetheless, the differences of opinion did not damage the bonds among the compatriots, and if it was a question of defending the national honor, whenever and wherever that might be, they all stood united.

For this reason, during the Chilean national holiday in September, the bikers of the Yugoslav colony won over the Spanish, Swiss, German, and Italian teams. Jakov Pesutić came in first, greatly outdistancing even his own teammates, and far ahead of the Spaniard Plácido Fernández and the Swiss Luis Salles. But the applause of the spectators and the tunes of the regimental band did not altogether drown out occasional resentful shouts of "Austrian shitheads!"

Kum Jakov posed for the photographers next to his bike, twisting his thin, bristly mustache. His eyes were flashing and he tried to smile. After the brief ceremony during which they pinned a medal on his jersey, he turned to my father: "They're still calling us 'Austrian shitheads.'"

"If they called you 'Yugoslav shithead' it would amount to the same thing. They're yelling at you because you won. An insult is the same whether you're Austrian or Yugoslav."

The festivities lasted the entire afternoon in both the Yugoslav and Dalmatian Clubs. One of "ours" had won. That was cause for celebration!

The next day my father commented: "The truth is we're all alike. We like to argue. We like to tease one another, without meaning any harm. We're stubborn and we always believe the other guy to be wrong. Since he thinks the same way, the discussion invariably winds up at the point where it began. But in the meantime we all spent a few hours together—hours that might otherwise have been very dull. That's how we are... and maybe that explains why our people have been able to do all the things it has done: to stop the Asiatic invaders, to defend the entire European culture, and to survive from the time of the Romans until now."

He cleared his throat and, to our surprise, continued: "The island of Brać, our island, and the coast of Dalmatia are full of very ancient ruins. There the Roman emperors before and after Diocletian built fortresses and monuments. That's how far Attila advanced with his hordes, and that's where he was driven back. That's where Dalmatian blood checked the barbarians and saved world civilization. I was born and I grew up among those ruins, and I carry something of all of that in my veins. For a people that go back many centuries, everything is transitory. Just yesterday it was the Austro-Hungarian Empire with all its splendor and immense, seemingly indestructible, power; today it is a new nation, hesitant, lacking direction, its future uncertain."

"What will happen tomorrow? The present changes. The future will be different. Only the past is unalterable. We're headed toward the future, but we come from the past. That means some part of us will always remain unchanged, and everything that is to come will be built on this immutable base."

It wasn't easy to follow this reasoning, but I tried to understand or at least remember these words. Lucho was pensive. Mama nodded in assent. Who, if not she, could understand him?

I went to bed strangely confused and had a hard time staying asleep. I dreamed that King Alexander[68] stepped out of his portrait and, using the scissors with which my mother cut our hair, trimmed Emperor Francis Joseph's sideburns. Francis Joseph was roaring with laughter.

***

At the Colegio San José I began to get to know my schoolmates by their last names, because the teachers, priests or not, called the roll every morning. They droned:

"Aguirre, Alvarez, Arbunić..."

Every nationality was represented: Italians, gringos,[69] Swiss, French, Scandinavians, "Turks,"

---

[68] King Alexander I of Yugoslavia (1929–1934) and before that king of the Serbs, Croats, and Slovenes (1921–1929).
[69] In this case, the sons of Englishmen.

Greeks, Spaniards, Chilotes, and "Austrians" like ourselves. The year whizzed past. The following year my younger brothers, too, came to San José, so our circle of friends grew larger every day. Talking to our classmates we found out whose store was the best, who was the best blacksmith or the best baker, who sold the nicest toys or made the best shoes, and where you could get stuff most cheaply—in short, all the things kids tell each other and accept as the absolute truth.

And so our carefree school years flew by.

In the meantime, however, things happened in the family. My father obtained large road-building contracts. Lucho, prompted by his innate restlessness, went off to work on large estancias; that was his world, that's where he felt in his element. The grocery store expanded, and Mama found it very difficult to run it by herself during my father's long absences, when he had to camp with his workmen many kilometers out of town.

By the time I was twelve I had to keep the books of our business and made mistakes on more than one occasion. But providentially my father always returned in time to solve the problem. He would smile understandingly and remark: "You'll get the hang of it! For the time being, do the best you can."

On my fourteenth birthday my father took me aside. "You're almost a man now. About some topics your teachers have taught you things I don't I know. But remember, I have lived longer than they have. If I give you advice, it's so you can avoid the errors I committed. Don't be arrogant, but don't be so humble that anyone feels free to step on you. Most importantly: be tolerant. If someone offends you without cause, give him a good slap. But if they offend you out of ignorance, forgive them and, above all, put the whole matter behind you. Forgiveness without forgetting is no forgiveness at all."

We were in the grocery store. It was afternoon, and the boy who usually brought the paper *El Magallanes* arrived. He was about eleven, with a shy but honest expression on this pale face; his clothes were mended but clean. My father absentmindedly handed him a twenty-cent piece and started to settle down to read the paper.

"See you tomorrow, sir."

"Wait a sec, young fellow!"

The boy stopped on the threshold; the little bell above the door tinkled.

"Do you know how to read?"

"No, sir; I've never gone to school."

"Would you like to go?"

"Yes, sir; but we're so poor..."

"What do you do all day long, besides selling the newspaper?"

"Nothing much. I help my mother a little, but other than that..."

"You really want to go to school?"

"Yes, sir."

"Hold on!"

My father got up and went to the breakfront where all sorts of things were kept. He took out three notebooks, a blackboard, a pencil, and a used spelling book. "What's your name?"

"Raúl. Raúl Barrientos."

"Here you go. The notebooks are new; so are the pencil and the blackboard. The spelling book was used by three of my sons, but it'll do the trick for you as well. Be here tomorrow at eight in the morning. I'm going to sign you up at Cerro de la Cruz, School Number Three."

And Raúl Barrientos attended school. What's more, he became the school's best student. He continued to bring the paper for my father in the afternoons, and it became my job to help him with his homework, sitting right at the counter of the Tres Estrellas.

That's what he was like, my Austro-Yugoslav father.

And that's what—in essence—all the men who had come from afar were like. They always talked about returning to their native land, but they always postponed their departure for a thousand different reasons. They alleged that it was winter there now; that their children were very small or that they were expecting a new baby and that such a trip would be too taxing for a pregnant woman; that at present there were few boats making the trip, but that one day the Panama Canal would get clogged with sand and then the ships of the whole world would have to resume their itinerary through the Strait of Magellan; that they had to fulfill a contract; that they first had to pay off a debt; that... any pretext that convinced no one.

Some—a minority—preferred to avoid the question and, in the end, when pressed for their decision, answered vaguely: "I think I couldn't get used to wearing *opanke* again or to go back to celebrating Christmas in wintertime."

Few, very few indeed, said firmly that they would remain in their children's homeland. Yet all of them, without a doubt, knew that this was how it had to be. They had come, nursing the illusion of becoming wealthy, to live the American dream.

"America took hold of us and won't let us go," as my father said. "It didn't shower us with riches, except in very few cases; on the other hand, it did cost us a lot of hard work and much suffering; but it also gave us the joy of seeing the birth of our children and the hope that we would see them grow and prosper. What more can we ask, if America also gives us freedom and peace?"

When someone objected that the climate was too inhospitable, my father answered: "A mild climate turns people into weaklings. We are a strong race. This rude climate is made to measure for us. Look at this city. It's lovely. Our houses are sturdy to withstand the wind, insulated to protect us from the cold, spacious so we won't feel stifled when the bad weather keeps us indoors; they're painted in cheerful colors to dispel gloom. Everything is close at hand: lumber from the woods, water from rivers that never dry up. And there's coal and gold. Maybe there's lots of coal and little gold, but we have both resources in the right amount for our needs. What good it would do to have gold in abundance, and not enough coal to heat our stoves during the icy days of winter? It all confirms my belief that He who created the world knew very well what He was doing, and He knew it so well, that He made us come here; and not only us, the Dalmatians; He also sent Spaniards, Germans, Swiss, Turks, and Jews."

One afternoon when Papa was holding forth in this manner in presence of Barba Jule and Don Pedro, the baker, the conversation turned to the past. Barba Jule had worked with my father in the gold-bearing sands of Tierra del Fuego and Navarino. That day he took the opportunity to tell us many things we didn't know, things my father had avoided to mention, possibly thinking us too young or simply because he disliked talking about failures.

Barba Jule became more and more animated— his eyes lit up and his smile was no longer timid—the farther he got into his narrative. "I'll never forget this storm! Even the captain, Pascuale Rispoli, known as 'Pascualini'—an eccentric prankster, brave to the point of recklessness—was afraid. We had left the Magdalena Channel around nine o'clock at night, when suddenly a rainstorm attacked us with relentless fury. We had to sail around Cape Brecknock and into the open sea. It was a grade 8 storm. The schooner had a full cargo; on deck we tried to hold onto the masts, the wheelhouse, the ropes—anything. There were twenty of us, bound for different points on Navarino Island. It was beastly cold and the night was pitch black. The deluge of freezing rain soaked us to the skin. We could barely breathe. The ship was rocking perilously and creaked all over, as if it were about to burst asunder. With the bow turned into the wind, our vessel rose and pitched, giving us the sensation that we might go to the bottom at any moment. To make matters worse, one man cried out to God begging for forgiveness for his sins. Something started to bang against the hull, making an awful racket. The captain, blaspheming in Italian, seized a hatchet and crawled to the bow so as to cut the anchor rope. The noise stopped. Those were moments when we wouldn't have bet even a cigarette butt for our lives.

"Do you remember, kume?"

"*Bogami, mierda!* That crazy fool pulled a quick one on us. He had overloaded the schooner and took as many people on board as he felt like... we almost didn't make it."

"But make it we did, and for months we worked like beasts from sunup to sundown, or, to be precise, from daylight to dusk, because the sun rarely appeared. Standing in almost freezing water, we altered the course of rivers, moved mountains of rocks and debris with shovels and pickaxes, constructed wooden conduits, and trapped the fine gold dust with mercury. Now, after so many years, all this is easy enough to tell, but in order to know what it was like, you had to have lived it. We—your father, Marco Martinić, and I—stayed on that island one whole year, enduring the most miserable climate in the world. It rained, it snowed, it hailed in a rapid succession of squalls—one day I counted over forty in one single day. When the precipitation was heavier than usual, the *piques*[70] got flooded; the swollen river carried off the work of entire weeks. Confined to our miserable shacks made out of trunks and *champas*,[71] we waited for the storm to blow over, drinking coffee, smoking, and playing cards. As soon as the weather improved slightly, we returned to our drudgery, once again standing in the water, to shovel sand and rocks, shaking the *chayas*,[72] handling the dangerous mercury, and, with tremendous sacrifices,

---

[70] Narrow trenches.
[71] Clumps of tall dry grass found in Patagonia.
[72] Primitive wooden dish used to pan for gold.

gathering the minuscule nuggets, one by one, in small glass flasks.

"There were three of us in each camp. A threesome is best when people have to spend so much time isolated from the rest of the world. If one of the group gets sick, there are always two to divvy up the countless tasks: preparing food, keeping the fire stoked, washing clothes, baking bread, sharpening and setting out the tools, watching day and night over the work, gauging the flow of the water, gathering the 'harvest,' and so on. In case of a disagreement, there's always one to arbitrate and find a solution."

"Although we didn't have a really bad time, things didn't go as smoothly as we had hoped either. There were mishaps, especially at the beginning of winter, when, in spite of all precautions, our supplies got wet and we were left without flour, pasta, or sugar. There was nothing for it—we were forced to look for help in the other camps. To get to them, we had to make our way along the seashore. It was a narrow strip of sand, blocked at times by enormous rocks, or intersected by swamps at the mouths of streamlets. The trip was strenuous, because the terrain was unknown to us and we didn't have any idea how far we would have to go before finding any of the others. Nor could we venture inland and climb the hills; the snow was treacherous, covering swamps, ravines, and underbrush and forming deadly traps."

Barba Jule downed his glass in one gulp, allowing my father to throw in a comment: "More than once I thought I would never again see Jule and Marko Martinić. They were gone for six days and I was at the camp by myself, biting my fingernails. On the third day I was tempted to set out after them, but it was my duty to guard our possessions. I slept with the Winchester and my revolver handy. The dangers were many: Yagan Indians might come by sea. They were always out and about in their canoes fishing and stealing whatever they could find. They don't know the meaning of bad weather; they're such excellent sailors they could navigate at night as well as during the day. They carry fire in a piece of turf or a bit of sand in the bottom of their boat; while the woman rows, the man fishes, armed with a harpoon or a crude net and a fishhook made of bone."

"Yes," said Barba Jule, taking up his narration once more. "That was one danger, but much worse were the adventurers who crossed the Beagle Channel: sea lion trappers and beaver hunters of diverse nationalities who were real pirates. Well armed and accustomed to kill Indians, they had no scruples about killing anyone, especially if they suspected he might carry some gold. This meant that Martinić and I were apprehensive as we made our cumbersome way from camp to camp, asking for some sugar at one, some flour at the next, and some rice even farther on, then loading the provisions into canvas bags that we lugged on our backs. At night we hung the bags from trees, to avoid the damp ground, and crouched around the fire until daybreak. It's impossible to forget any of this, but, hell, we were young and wanted to get rich quickly, even if it meant risking our lives."

"As it turned out, we came back as poor as we had set out, because in mid-autumn, just when we expected our best 'harvest', Pascualini's schooner appeared at the mouth of the river. The Italian had already picked up all the other miners from the island and urged us to embark. There was no alternative. We had to abandon everything and go on board. There would be no other ship until next year. In a couple of hours we stashed away our tools and wooden gutters in the shack, gathered our clothes and the flasks, which, in the course of a whole year, we never did manage to fill up with gold, and left Navarino with the firm intention to return in the spring. Actually, we never did. It just wasn't profitable. All the gold we collected barely sufficed to cover the costs of the expedition."

"That's life, kume. Had we gone back we might have stayed in Navarino forever with a few bullet holes in our backs."

"But that doesn't mean that we didn't get involved in even worse adventures: hunting foxes and guanacos for their skins in Tierra del Fuego, the most inhospitable place in the world. There everyone drove his own team of horses to open a path in the snow, taking shelter under a *calafate*[73]—covered with pieces of canvas or a blanket to serve as an awning—and spent days at a time in mortal anguish, surrounded by nothing but the white steppe dying in the far horizon against a gray sky. Always with a weapon at the ready, fearing an attack of the roving Onas or, what was even worse, afraid of being buried forever under the snow that often fell softly and inexorably for weeks on end. When the provisions gave out, we would have to shoot a vulture, pluck its feathers, and hang the carcass from a tree so that the sight of its black, scrawny hard flesh would attract others of its species. That's what we would eat, birds of prey, barely cooked over a fire of green branches. We had to melt snow in a pot to make coffee and, for sure, give up all thoughts of enjoying our daily bread.

"The skins were profitable; the greatest difficulty was to transport them. Ten or twelve horses were barely enough; we had to cover hundreds of kilometers, going back and forth for months, and in the end we had to find a ship to cross the Strait to get back to Punta Arenas."

"While you're young and don't have family obligations, everything goes smoothly," added my father. "But once you get hitched, everything turns complicated."

---

[73] Thorny bush of Patagonia that produces blue berries in the summer.

- 153 -

"We were never sure we'd make it back," threw in Barba Jule. "In the end you figure that it's not worth risking your neck for four crazy pesos that slip out of your hands without your even knowing how or when. Sometimes I asked myself why in the hell I didn't simply gather up my stuff and return to my country; but somehow, I don't know why, I kept on staying. Until I married my Dorina. Then my daughters were born, three of them, one after the other, each year more or less on the same date. To live and support them, I worked all kinds of jobs. I sowed potatoes and cabbages; I sheared sheep on the large estancias; I became a cabbie; I opened a *boliche* and now, finally, a bakery."

Don Pedro, the "baker"—really a bread distributor rather than a bread maker—said: "It's good business. People can do without potatoes and cabbage, but they can't do without bread."

Barba Jule's eyes lit up with pleasure. "When my bakery gets to be as big as that of Marusić, where you are now working, I'll hire you to distribute my bread. You'll have a blue cart with a sign saying "Bakery Dalmatia;" it will be pulled by a white horse with jingle bells on its harness."

***

We received sad news: the lovely Antonia, the girl with the beauty spot on her cheek, had died. My mother started to cry and crossed herself. My father chewed on

- 154 -

his *toscano* and mumbled something we couldn't make out, probably a blasphemy; then he, too, grimly crossed himself and abruptly disappeared into the bedroom. He came back shortly afterward, dressed in his black Sunday suit: "I'm going to the wake. 'Meštre'[74] Mote might need some help."

My mother served us supper in silence and had us kneel by our beds to pray for the soul of the dead girl. I was now fourteen years old and felt like rebelling, but didn't want to set a bad example for my younger brothers. So I stayed on my knees until they stopped hurting. My mother recited some long prayers in her native language and we responded, "Amen." The little ones went to sleep without my noticing that they had gone to bed.

When they carried the white coffin out of "Meštre" Mote's house, I couldn't contain my tears. From inside the house came the heartrending laments of the mother—whom I remembered as the smiling and chatty lady of former days—and that of the other women, young and old, who were keeping her company. The coffin was carried by six youths, barely older than me, who wore white ribbons on their left sleeves. In front walked a priest reading a little black book and an acolyte carrying the cross; behind followed the father, the godparents and

---

[74] Literally "master," in this context, someone excelling at his trade.

relatives, and finally a motley crowd of friends and neighbors.

Their steps resounded on the pavement like a murmur. No one spoke, and almost everybody hung their heads, as if they were counting the cobblestones that my father and his compatriots had aligned so expertly and laboriously. On our long walk to the cemetery I couldn't help thinking that one day we too would have to be carried along these streets, along which we so cheerfully walked every day—asleep forever, our feet not touching the ground.

Within the cemetery's solid gray walls and monumental entrance with its vaulted ceiling as magnificent as a cathedral, was the biggest and most beautiful garden I had ever seen. To the right there were mausoleums—splendid as palaces—with elaborate bronze doors, granite columns, and angels of white marble and elegant gilt crosses. The avenues were of fine white sand, edged by masterfully pruned conical cypresses; larger branches at the top waved in the breeze like the plumes of a military guard. To the left, where our procession was heading, there was nothing to bar our view of the clear blue sky. It was the small world of the children.

The mourners' sad expressions seemed out of place in such beautiful surroundings. Brightly colored wreaths of paper flowers, hanging from plain white wooden crosses and filigreed enclosures marking off small well-kept plots, seemed like a gentle invitation to the enchanted kingdom that the beautiful blonde girl with the large silk bow in her hair would inhabit. The presence of death was palpable only in the whispered prayers of the priest and the restrained silence of everyone else.

I didn't go near the grave. I shuddered when I heard the clods of earth thudding on the coffin lid as the priest intoned: "Requiescat in pace!"

"Amen."

Walking next to Dr. Béncur and my father, with whose large strides I could now keep up, we reached the top of the Cerro de la Cruz. We stopped to look at the sunset, aware of sharing the same sad thoughts.

"She was a lovely girl," said my father almost in a whisper. "In a few years you might have become engaged to each other." He spoke without looking at me, his gaze fixed in the distance where one could make out the bluish coastline of Tierra del Fuego. "Right?"

"Yes."

"Or was she your sweetheart already?"

"Yes."

He took out a *toscano*, bit off its tip, spitting it out angrily, and lit up with a trembling hand. A moment later he placed his hand on my shoulder and murmured in a choked-up voice: "Let's go, my son."

"Dying is natural, like being born... provided one has had a chance to live. But here too many are dying at a very young age. There's hardly a family that doesn't have two or three children in this most beautiful and most terrible cemetery. Half the graves belong to children."

Dr. Béncur looked at my father. "No need to tell me about that. I sign death certificates every day. Fortunately I have to do it less and less often every year. People are beginning to understand that when a kid gets sick, it's time to skip herbs and quackery and call a physician instead. This climate tends to cause rickets and tuberculosis; besides, hardly anybody knows how to eat the right diet or how to take preventative measures. There are entire families sick with consumption, condemned to die in the span of a few short years; yet their offspring marry freely, without any constraint—a real crime against themselves and future generations. We physicians try to teach, to prevent, and to cure; but there are few of us, and however hard we try, we can't perform miracles. Almost without exception, we are called when it's already too late. If I were to resign myself to this state of affairs, I'd become a gravedigger, instead of working as a doctor. But I see my mission differently and won't allow myself to give up; I know that a few years from now, as people learn certain basic norms, the situation is bound to improve. I am completely convinced that the children of your children will be healthy and strong as oaks. And if I'm wrong in this, let me cease being who I am!"

Perhaps time would vindicate Dr. Mateo Béncur; but in spite of the strength of the doctor's faith in a brighter tomorrow, my father, like the rest of his compatriots, could not dispel his doubts, and one could hear many anxious words spoken concerning their children.

Consumption caused the death of five of my classmates that year. In our neighborhood, wakes for "the little angels" were commonplace. Chilote households did a flourishing business from the sale of tissue paper wreaths; some women earned a living chanting and wailing from wake to wake; and the stern gravedigger, with a lawyer's perspicacity, kept track of the deceased. To see him drive through the streets, perched on the driver's seat of his third-rate black-and-white-striped carriage, pulled by an emaciated horse, his hat pulled down over his eyes and his chin sunk onto his chest, was a daily and familiar occurrence no longer frightening anybody. Rather than death's coachman, he seemed a passing visitor who some day, sooner or later, would have to stop briefly in front of our door as well.

Cod-liver oil was the panacea, and at our house we consumed it by the liter. A huge spoonful before each meal left such an unpleasant taste in our mouths that we would have swallowed just about anything as long as it would mask that bad flavor. Maybe this was Dr. Béncur's whole secret: to get us to eat. But how would this work with those who had nothing, except for a piece of bread and some boiled potatoes?

As my father said, the cemetery continued to be the most beautiful and the most terrible in the entire world.

***

How rapidly time went by! It seemed that classes had just begun, and here we were approaching the end of the year, with the painful commotion of final examinations.

"Exam" was a weighty word in the Colegio San José for those of us studying humanities. Even our teachers trembled. The law decreed that our exams had to be presided over by commissions formed by teachers from the public high school. All of these teachers were steeped in radical, masonic, anticlerical sectarianism. So in some ways the exam was more like an execution, or, at least, refined torture. At the end of November we began to make appropriate vows to the Virgen del Carmen, St. Anthony, St. Joseph, and all the other important saints who graced the altars of the cathedral. Since these penuries coincided with the Month of Mary, little altars were erected in every classroom, in the hallways, in the school courtyard, and in every pupil's house. People were vying with each other to put up decorations, candles, and flowers.

"Venid y vamos todos,
con flores a porfía,
con flores a María,
que madre nuestra es."

[Come and let's all join in,
with flowers to the faithful,
with flowers to Mary,
who is our Mother.]

My father managed to look calmer than he felt; he knew, as always, how to encourage us by pretending that he considered the entire matter a joke. However, it was a fact that one of my brothers was held back a year, primarily because his fear had prevented him from uttering a single word when facing the examining commission.

The distribution of our ages in the various grades allowed my father to toy with the numbers: "My first son is in third grade," he would say. "The third, in second; the second and the fourth, in first; and the fifth—since he is the last—is in the fourth."[75]

We were lucky enough to pass the exams. My mother claimed we owed it to her novenas to the Holy Mother of God; but my father evidently was not so sure that her prayers alone were responsible. He rather thought that we had succeeded thanks to his strict supervision of our studies. No doubt both were right.

Vacations!

***

They would have been lovely vacations had it not occurred to my father to bring me—as a sort of prize—some books on navigation. After dinner, when the late afternoon beckoned me to come outside to play ball, I had to sit at the table while my father explained nautical terms to me: beam, length, height; portside, starboard, day's run and course, rigging, shrouds, topsails, topgallant sails; keel, helm; windward and leeward; to lie to and "get under weigh."

Sundays he rouse me at dawn to take me to the bay. From the pier or from the beach he made me watch the ships and asked me questions that at times drove me to despair. But I ended up learning and, what's more, becoming enthusiastic about maritime matters. We frequently rode the motor launch *Alice*, which transported

---

[75] In Chile at the time education was divided into six basic (preparatory) grades and six secondary (humanities) grades.

passengers between the pier and the ships; standing on its small deck, we defied the wind and the heavy seas.

One day we climbed down into the engine room of a huge English freighter. Below sea level the deafening racket of the crankshafts, the infernal heat of the boilers, the loud shouts of the officers and their boatswains, the strength of the men, the narrow corridors, the vertical metal ladders all seemed part of a strange and fascinating world of shattering noise, sweat, shouts, and fatigue. When we got back on deck the fresh air felt chilly and I started to shiver.

***

The first thing I noticed was a triangle with its point facing down. Then a pair of bright eyes lit up, and now I clearly recognized the well-shaped beard of Dr. Béncur.

"He came through it all right! I'll be back tomorrow. Give him a pill every three hours." And he added with satisfaction: "The boy is out of danger."

"Thanks to the Virgen del Carmen," murmured my mother.

"And to Dr. Béncur," added my father.

"Not to mention the cod-liver oil," said the doctor, as he put on his rustling raincoat and pulled his hat down to his ears.

I recuperated quickly. After all, I had things to do. I was needed in the neighborhood soccer games. The team from our street—Balmaceda—had lost two matches, and the teams from Peruana and Arauco Streets were serious rivals. Moreover, three blocks down the hill lived the Arancibia sisters, and I liked one of them quite a bit. So one week later, my shins already bruised from kicks received in a ball game, I limped down the three blocks to hold hands with Isabel while her sisters looked at the moon.

The calm of those serene summer nights was broken only by the distant barking of dogs and the occasional spluttering of a motorcar. Now there was automobile traffic in all parts of town and the bright headlights made it more difficult to steal a kiss. How I missed the weak paraffin lamps you could snuff out with one breath! Electricity was repulsive! Although we had become experts at breaking streetlights with our slingshots, our joy didn't last long: the next day the bulbs were replaced. Haven't the municipal workers ever been young?

6

EVERYTHING IN ITS PLACE

We liked to go to Tía Keka's house. She too had five sons, and when we ten cousins got together, the earth started trembling. Of the five "Kekinos" at least three wanted to become pirates and the other two were almost pirates already. All they needed was a ship. So we decided to build one.

We did this in our patio because it was larger and essential supplies were at hand there. Since I had been initiated in nautical matters, I assumed the title of "naval engineer" and sketched the plans on a piece of cardboard.

The ship was seven meters long—the length of two ladders used to climb on the roof to clean the chimney or sweep off the snow. It was a bit more than a meter in breadth and about ninety centimeters in height. The sides were lined with empty wheat and potato sacks from the storeroom. We constructed a jaunty smokestack from long strips of tin that once had been part of the kitchen stove. Various empty boxes formed the superstructure; the cabins consisted of sacks spread on the ground.

Since a boat has to give off smoke, we used a paraffin can as a firebox and mounted the smokestack on top of it. The ship also had a rudder, which we patiently manufactured from a barrel lid and several strips of wood laid across it, leaving eight points jutting out. Except for the inherent aberrations, ours was as good a ship as any other. We painted on beards and mustaches with burnt cork, tied kerchiefs around our heads, and stuck patches over one eye. We were pirates!

But the big moment came when we lit the fire and "went to sleep" in our "cabins." Since the smokestack was merely decorative, the smoke could not escape from it; instead it lingered "below deck," forcing us to "abandon ship," coughing, half suffocated, eyes watering. Mama seemed highly alarmed, but my father roared with laughter, exclaiming: "You sure are a fine bunch of sailors!"

And while we spluttered and dried our tears, he added: "Everything in its place. A ship, to be a ship, has to be in the water; and a man, to be a man, has to know what he's doing." And, still laughing, he went indoors.

The ship morphed back into ladders, sacks, and boxes. We washed our faces and went back to being kids.

***

My mother knelt on the floor, a bucket next to her, and scrubbed the floor with a stiff brush and soapy water. Like most of her compatriots she took great pride in the cleanliness of her home. Cleaning was the most arduous and basic of her many daily tasks: to do the laundry; to iron, mend, and set out our clothes for the next day; to bake bread and to fix the meals—breakfast, lunch, afternoon coffee and supper. But that was not all. She took care of the chickens, the dog, the cat, and the singing goldfinch in its little red cage, tended the small vegetable plot for cabbages and lettuce, and kept plants in pots and painted boxes indoors on the windowsills along the passageway, where she grew hollyhocks, roses, carnations, geraniums, hydrangeas, and fuchsias, as well as basil and salvia. She also made sure the curtains on all the windows were immaculate, even those on the windows overlooking the patio, and that there were knitted embroidered doilies placed under every vase and a cushion on every one of our hard chairs.

Mama's day started at four in the morning and didn't end until nine at night. And what's more: when Papa went out, she had to mind the grocery store as well and—if we happened to be involved in some neighborhood mischief—listen to the other parents' complaints. But even with all that, she managed to find time to rush out to help a sick relative or fellow Dalmatian by tidying up their house and preparing the diet recommended by the physician; she attended baptisms, first communions, and weddings; she went to matins every Sunday, and on November evenings during the Month of Mary, she was in church to recite the rosary. Furthermore, it was Mama who took us downtown to buy shoes, clothes, and books.

She was a slight woman, but she was tough. She had a sweet smile but a strong character. It was amazing to hear her sing all day while performing her endless chores. We felt respect and affection for our father, but it was our mother who earned our love and tenderness.

One day my father insisted that she accept the help of Fat Rosalía, Oyarzún's stepdaughter. I think my mother at first felt slightly dethroned, but after she had followed Rosalía for several days into the remotest corners of the house to keep tabs on her, Mama seemed satisfied with her performance and returned to her knitting and embroidery and to her old hand-wheel sewing machine. She replenished our supply of shirts and underwear and even made a new canvas bag for Zvonko.

At Tía Keka's, Kuma[76] Dorina's, Doña Lucía's, and Doña Franka's one could observe the same commotion, the same concerns, and the same exertions. The women paid each other frequent visits, especially if there was some "news" to be shared. Christian charity didn't always reign during these get-togethers, but they had their positive side: delicious sweets were served, and precious reminiscences about the distant homeland made the rounds.

Once a year all the mattresses were overhauled. For this task the women picked days at the end of January or the beginning of February when the weather was more or less stable. Each woman completed the first part of the job by herself: she emptied, washed, and set out to dry the wool from the casings of the family mattresses. And if washing the woolen stuffing was laborious, drying it was actually risky business. The wet wool was spread out on the roof of the henhouse and covered by pieces of mesh wire, weighted down by a few logs or rocks, to prevent it from being blown away by the wind. Here's where we kids came in: if a squall seemed in the offing, we had to scamper up onto the roof and hurriedly gather up all the wool; and we had to repeat this operation every evening in case it should rain during the night. So drying the wool might take anywhere from three

---

[76] Godmother.

to fifteen days. An additional week was needed to hand-card the wool. All the while we had to sleep on the bare box springs, which had bumps in the most bothersome places.

Finally the day came to restuff the mattresses. In high spirits, talking, joking, and laughing, all the women gathered around the dining room table. Equipped with special huge needles and skeins of hemp, they skillfully rebuilt each mattress, leaving it springy, soft, and warm.

Day after day, the women moved from house to house, repeating this same task, but didn't seem any more tired than if they had just been to a wonderful party. It was at these gatherings that they planned many future summer outings to the nearby countryside.

Picking wild strawberries was something special that occurred at most twice or three times every summer. Yet no summer went by without berrying. Since the picking season coincided with our vacations, we participated in every one of these excursions. Four or five women from the old country set out, accompanied by all those of their children capable of walking and taking care of their "business." It seemed like a small exodus: all of us kids, girls and boys, in the lead, jumping ditches and fences; all the mothers in the rear, moving at a more dignified pace, engaged in lively conversation. Everyone, without exception, carried a basket or an empty can with a wire handle. We older ones also had to lug all the stuff for our luncheon: cold cuts, bread, cakes, soft drinks, and a few bottles of wine mixed with water. After walking a couple of hours we reached the wild strawberry patches and separated into small groups to start picking. There were a few problems: usually those who went picking for the first time collected only a few green berries, squashing the ripe ones between their fingers. The tasty, bright red berries were hard to detect, because they were covered by lush green leaves that formed a dense carpet at ground level. You had to learn, first of all, how to spot them and, next, how to get at them gently from below, by digging into the sandy soil.

We spent tiring hours bending over a thousand times until we had filled our basket or can; then, famished as field hands, we devoured our lunch. Out in the open, next to a stream gurgling at the bottom of a ravine or squirting down the cliffs in fine jets, our meal seemed delicious.

A bit later, we sang as we walked down from the hills back toward the distant city, spread out by the sea.

Along the road we met carters returning to the hills to spend the night in their huts made of logs and *champas*. The next morning they would be back in the town below, delivering loads of lumber and wood charcoal. It was the hour when dairy farmers briefly let the calves suckle their mothers in the stables and the echo carried their lowing and the dogs' barking all around. In the foliage you could hear trills, calls, and the flapping of wings.

We jumped over the same ditches and scrambled over the same fences; and as we were walking through the fields, the women stuck blossoms of wildflowers in their hair or gathered them into exquisite bouquets. When we got home, we wanted nothing but to sleep off the fatigue and get rid of the burning sensation on our faces, caused by long hours in the sun and the open air. But our exertions were well rewarded: for many weeks we would feast on the delicious jam that Mama prepared for us in her large cast iron cauldron.

That's how it was every summer. In addition to the wild strawberries, there were the *calafate*s that left your mouth black and your hands full of scratches from the tenacious protection of their spiny branches. Their small dark berries were as sweet as grapes, though, and their red juice could be fermented to produce an inebriating wine, always kept handy by woodcutters, carters, and charcoal burners.

Another thing you had to experience at least once every season was a good *asado*. Since it was mostly the men, rather than the women, who did the grilling, and the preparations took a long time, *asados* could be scheduled on Sundays only.

A week prior to one such *asado*, my father started informing his customers that the grocery would be closed the following Sunday. Kum Jakov selected two of the best *chiporros*[77] from his butcher shop. The women prepared salads, cakes, biscuits, and special bread.

That Sunday my father woke me before dawn. It was cold. For the first time in my life he gave me a sip of *rakija*. It burned my mouth and throat, but it warmed me up. The counter and the floor of the grocery were covered with baskets containing everything required, from the matches to the dessert. While we children were asleep, our parents had worked until late and Kum Jakov had brought over the two lambs. Among the forest of those wickerwork baskets one could make out a large demijohn holding eighteen liters of good red wine, a case of beer, and an ample supply of lemonade. Papa was impatient.

Oyarzún arrived in the chill clarity of dawn riding his squealing cart. Then Kum Jakov appeared followed by his oldest son—nose and hands red from the morning cold. The water was boiling on the stove, and Mama came in hurriedly to prepare substantial mugs of coffee and to butter slices of fresh bread.

Soon afterward we heard the clatter of hooves and the sound of Barba Jule's light carriage rolling over the pavement. He brought his entire family, poor in boys and rich in girls of various ages. Kum Ivon in his sulky, accompanied by his three daughters, pulled up next, to

---

[77] Lambs that are less than one year old.

be followed shortly by Kum Grgo with his girls. Seeing ourselves outnumbered by all these females, we anxiously awaited the arrival of Tía Keka's male reinforcements. My mother, shrewdly assessing the situation, hurried to get my brothers out of bed.

Kum Jakov, his eldest son, my father and I climbed into Oyarzún's cart, where all the supplies had been stashed, and off we went in a cloud of cigar smoke. The sun was rising out of the sea, tingeing the sky red. My father forecast a fine day.

It took Oyarzún's slow-paced oxen almost two hours to reach the designated spot. Kum Ivon and Barba Jule caught up with us, despite having set out much later. They discharged their passengers and promptly turned back to town to pick up the remaining women and the younger children.

Oyarzún, whose cabin was nearby, brought logs and built a wonderful fire, while Kum Jakov skewered the *chiporros* on the spits and rubbed the meat down with his "secret" sauce, whose formula he was planning to pass on to his firstborn only on his own deathbed.

When the rest of the company arrived an hour later, breakfast was served, consisting of coffee, sweets, and sandwiches with cold cuts, after which we boys went to play ball and the girls to jump rope.

The instant Kum Jakov announced the *asado* was done, there we were ready for it, plates in hand. Seeking shade under the oaks and shelter from the wind near the *calafate* bushes, we clustered in cheerful groups. On the sly, we poured much more wine than lemonade into our jars. Our peals of laughter, multiplied by the echo, resounded in the woods.

Kum Ivon went to his sulky, pulled a suitcase from under the seat, and took out an accordion. He installed himself on a fallen tree and tried the first measures: "Tamo daleko, daleko kraj mora..."

Soon everybody had gathered around him, men and women, singing at the top of their voices. They moved from one song to the next, going through the whole repertory several times, until they were hoarse and Kum Ivon was tired. It was time for a nice siesta on the fragrant grass.

Only Oyarzún stayed by the fire, parsimoniously cutting off thin slices of *asado* and, once in a while, taking a swig from the jar. He would wipe his mustache on his sleeve and calmly repeat the whole operation again and again. As a result, when the others woke from their nap, refreshed and ready to head home, Oyarzún was stretched out on the ground, sleeping like a log. My father and Barba Jule had to shake him awake and virtually drag him to his cabin.

I had never before been in the home of a woodcutter. It was a very narrow and dark place. The slanting walls, made out of wooden beams, met at the top, A-frame-style. The cracks were plastered with dry mud mixed with grass. Both the back and the front walls were made of turf bricks; the door was made of wooden planks, roughly fashioned by an axe. A few large rocks on the floor served as the hearth, its fire now extinguished. There was a small kettle and a teapot, blackened, like the walls, from years of accumulated soot. Oddly enough, there was no foul smell but rather the odor of cold smoke and the aromas of countless meals that had impregnated the timbers. Against the back wall stood a cot covered by several lambskins and two blankets that appeared to have been recently laundered.

When we came out into the open—having left Oyarzún on his cot, under a blanket—the sun caused me to blink. My father went to Oyarzún's cart and set his oxen free. Barba Jule and Kum Ivon got their carriages ready, the women and younger children climbed in, and they set off at a trot. The rest of us went on foot, singing cheerfully.

Never before had I been so struck by the grandeur of the scenery. The twisted trees bent eastward had almost no branches on the side exposed to the constant lashing of the west wind, to which they had been subjected from the time they were saplings. The underbrush, the *coirón*, and the flowers seemed to be bowed in prayer facing the sunrise. "They are like the 'Turks,'" said my father, "they look toward the Orient."

Papa had taught me that if you lose your bearings out in the wilds, all you have to do is to look in which direction the branches are bent. Hunters, herdsmen, wanderers, and petty traders had been saved by this unmistakable sign: the tops of trees protruding from deep snowdrifts in the endless whiteness, pointing toward the sunrise.

But now everything was glorious. The small brook flowed among the rocks murmuring quietly; collared sparrows, long-tailed meadow larks, and austral parakeets fluttered around in the foliage chattering diaphanously; the calafates shone like black pearls, and the fresh smell of the grass crushed by our steps mixed with the sylvan fragrance in the air.

The breeze, passing through the tightly strung wire fences, whistled gently, and everything seemed to form a chorus with our voices full of life and merriment.

We were in no hurry. We all seemed to want to prolong the peaceful mood of those moments when the setting sun stretched our shadows across the hillside.

My father mentioned countless times that this was a beautiful land, and no one cared to contradict him as his voice rose above all others accompanying him in a lively chorus, and repeating the naive refrain:

"Ti si Milko moja, moja,

ti si Milko moja, moja, moja.

Ja san tvoj,

ljubi Milko mene, mene, mene..."

[You are mine, Millie,

you are mine Millie.

I am yours,

love me, Millie, love me..."]

About that time Lucho returned and spent a few weeks at our house. He seemed a different person. He dressed elegantly and shaved every day. Every so often he brewed himself a few *mates* and proceeded to tell us what had happened to him with the characteristic gaiety and laughter that caused fine wrinkles to mark his virile features. He had encountered—how could it have been otherwise!—a number of amusing adventures, and he related them to us with good-humored charm.

He had worked as a kitchen boy on an Argentine estancia in Tierra del Fuego, near Río Grande. There the *peones*, the sheep herders, and the horse tamers thought of him the way kitchen boys are thought of, as someone good for nothing. Lucho, acting the fool, took it all as a private joke and bade his time.

One Sunday after lunch two of the best horse tamers met to settle a bet: which of them could break in "El Parchao,"[78] a beautiful snow-white colt with a black patch on his left shoulder. The colt had a history of catapulting a number of expert riders into the underbrush, head over heels, and, what's more, going after the unseated riders and attacking them with his hooves.

Barría, nicknamed "the Crooked," a fierce and agile Chilote and Pelegrini, a half-breed Tehuelche from Patagonia, got ready; they flipped a coin—heads or cross—to see who'd go first. Some fifty men had gathered around to watch. The Tehuelche Pelegrini approached slowly and carefully, while several *peones* held down the colt that was fighting fiercely to rid himself of the lasso. When Pelegrini got within about a meter and a half of the animal, he took a flying leap, grabbed hold of the mane, and swung himself onto the creature's back. The colt started bucking like a demon until he had thrown the Tehuelche, head first, onto the ground; Pelegrini, expert that he was, rolled out of reach of the animal's hooves.

Three or four gauchos set off at a gallop to round up the colt, and a few minutes later they had him tied up at the hitching rack again.

---

[78] Derived from *parche*, meaning "patch" in Spanish.

The Indian came back, limping. "Take care, Chilote! He's vicious. He starts to buck to the right and just when you think you've got him, bang! he switches to the left and hurls you to the ground."

They allowed some time for the animal to calm down, then it was Barría's turn. He was no luckier than the half-breed and broke a couple of ribs when he landed on the ground after being propelled forward over the colt's head.

Just then Don Tomás Pistinić, the manager of the estancia, appeared. He took out a bill of a hundred *nacionales* and placed it on one end of the hitching rack, weighing it down with a rock so the wind wouldn't carry it off. "Let's see, boys. Whoever's capable of snatching this bill while seated on El Parchao may keep both the money and the colt."

The men exchanged glances. The offer was tempting, but..."Lordy, Don Tomás," exclaimed one of the Chileans. "Open your wallet! Make that a thousand or at least five hundred, to pay for setting the bones afterward."

Don Tomás laughed. "Isn't there anyone who dares take me up on it?"

"I will!"

Seeing Lucho dressed in *bombachas* and short boots, *lloronas*[79] scraping the ground, there was a moment of silence, and then everybody burst out laughing at once.

Lucho, ignoring the laughter and the taunts, walked up to the horse from the front. He stretched out his hands to see if he would bite, but the animal merely jerked its head. He adroitly unhitched the horse, made him go in circles by pulling at the rope around his neck, and when El Parchao opened his mouth, Lucho cleverly inserted the rope as reins and made the horse turn and turn to make him a bit dizzy. Then, with an unexpected leap, Lucho was on his back, digging in his spurs, and when the colt threw back its head to break Lucho's face, Lucho gave him a ferocious blow between the ears and took off across the pampa like a fiend, belaboring his mount with his whip and his spurs, yelling savagely. Every time the beast tried to buck, Lucho let him have it with his whip and dug the sharp wheels of his spurs into his flanks, drawing blood. In this manner Lucho rode him more than a league, until horse and rider were lost from sight.

Lucho came back at a trot. He rode by the hitching rack, collected the hundred-peso bill and leaped

---

[79] Huge spurs, literally "weepers," after the noise they produce as the gaucho walks.

to the ground. "If you like, you can get on now, Don Tomás. He's gentler than a needy woman."

***

With El Parchao and a packhorse Lucho went off to shear sheep in various estancias around the island. Wherever he went, he made new friends: Spaniards, Italians, and Yugoslavs, almost all of them recently arrived from Europe in hopes of making a quick fortune in America. Only time would teach them that they already possessed a fortune: their life and their fortitude.

When the hard work was done and the southern winter manifested itself in icy sunrises and short afternoons, four Dalmatian men rode in silence across the endless expanse of the pampa. Behind them followed the packhorses and the dogs, tired and hungry.

They spotted a faint light in the distance. Could it be an estancia? Perhaps. But it was too far away for them to think of reaching it that night. They camped in the shelter of a thicket. After feeding the dogs their meat rations and drinking a mug of coffee, each of the men made a crude bed with his saddle and his horse blankets and covered himself with a piece of canvas.

Lucho woke up hot and sweaty. He knew what that meant: the snow that had fallen during the night had formed a light eiderdown on top of the canvas, keeping out the cold. He sat up carefully, rolling back his covers toward his feet. Snow was falling gently in very small flakes, and the sun was a reddish disk, barely visible through the gray clouds. Lucho looked for the previous night's extinguished campfire, where all the utensils had been left. He shook a few bushes, gathered some small dry branches, and soon had a fire going. Only then did he wake his neophyte companions, purposely letting them get snow into their clothes, faces, and eyes. "That's the way to learn," he commented.

The snow had effaced roads and paths, but, guided by the sun, they continued in the direction where they had made out the light at dusk the evening before.

That's how they chanced upon the Mission of the Salesian Fathers near Río Grande. There an Italian priest, ruddy and smiling, invited them in. They felt as if they hadn't eaten for a century and devoured the breakfast of cutlets, fried eggs, fresh bread, and *mate* cooked with milk, served by an Indian.

It was Sunday and Father Mario asked them—in order not to set a bad example for the *indiecitos*[80]—to attend Holy Mass in the chapel. He handed each a hymnal. The Indians, men and women, led by a layman, sang with deep and plaintive voices; the four visitors tried in vain to follow the insipid melody. Suddenly, when a long silence fell, Šime Eterović broke it with his mighty baritone:

---

[80] A slightly pejorative term for the Indians, referring to them as if they were children.

"Malena je Dalmacija,
al' je dika rodu svom... !"

[Dalmatia is small,
but its lineage is honorable… !]

And during the solemn moment of the Consecration, the wooden walls and the colored windowpanes shook from the spirited strains of a march issuing from four powerful throats:

"Stupaj naprid, sokole, sokole, sokole,
na talianske lopove, lopove, lopove."

[Onward, Falcons, Falcons, Falcons,
against the Italian bandits, bandits, bandits...]

"Whether the priest caught on," Lucho continued, "is something we never found out, because he served us a splendid luncheon and happily accepted our offer to carry a load of firewood into the kitchen. We were shown to comfortable beds, and on Monday at daybreak, when we were having coffee before our departure, he joined us with a bottle of the port he used for mass and had a long drink with us. We felt somewhat embarrassed, because no doubt we had gone a bit too far in church. But Father

Mario, with a mischievous glint in his eyes, said: 'Boys, may God be with you. May He bless you and preserve forever your cheerfulness, which is the best thing in this life and the next. Just imagine Heaven full of these sad Indians!'"

***

However much my father tried to talk Lucho into spending the winter with us, he couldn't persuade him, even when offering him a salary for working in the grocery store. Lucho was used to the freedom of the wind, the clouds, and the birds and, harnessing his team of horses, well provided with victuals, arms, and munition, he set out to "bring back fox pelts and guanaco skins."

"This wild son of mine... one day they're going to bring him to me slung across a saddle."

7

THE YEARS FLY BY

The whole house was saturated with wonderful smells. Once again my mother took cakes, biscuits, and sweet rolls out of the oven. The next day was St. Anthony's Day and there would be a party at the Dobronićes. To go empty-handed would have been unthinkable.

Behind the counter my father and I were going over old bills.

"Rómulo lost his son. He won't be able to pay. Tear up that bill."

Rómulo Mansilla's bill was entered as a loss.

"Old Candelaria is very sick. She's no longer able to take in laundry. Tear up that paper... But this one... leave this one to me, *bogami!* Even if a hundred years go by, I will get my money from him! He gave me his word and I will see that he keeps it."

The doorbell tinkled. In came a blast of cold air and, along with it, a martial figure. An officer with an impressive black mustache, golden laurels on his cap, pants with a broad red stripe, shiny boots, and a gilt saber entered, followed by a very young lieutenant with a red sash across his chest. My father drew himself up and clicked his heels. "Good afternoon, Colonel!"

"Good afternoon, sir! What a delicious smell!"

My father smiled with pleasure: "Would you care to try a sample? They're almond biscuits. They taste great with a glass of *rakija*."

A little while later the colonel, the lieutenant, and my father were sitting at the dining room table, talking animatedly, each sipping their glass of *rakija* and enjoying the sweets set out on a well-garnished tray. To tell the truth, the lieutenant was excluded from the conversation and only reached for the tray after his superior had done so, and then not even every time. He limited himself to assenting to the colonel's remarks with slight nods.

The discussion was about supplying the regiment for a campaign that was to last two months. The colonel wanted my father to draw up a proposal and gave him two weeks to submit it. My father agreed to study the matter and reply within a week. Then, after several more drinks, the conversation moved to other topics.

"Yes, Colonel: I served for four years in the Austro-Hungarian Navy. I rose to seaman first class. I instructed the cabin boys and the cadets, and in addition I was an artilleryman. The training voyage on board the *Saida*, an old wooden four-master, lasted more than three years. I still have the gold-lettered ribbon from my cap somewhere. We always had to navigate by sail because the engines broke down a lot and the coal bunkers were very small. All kinds of mishaps befell us: a fire broke out on board; we were becalmed for three agonizing months during which the sea made the vessel creak as if to take it to pieces, malnutrition begot all sorts of sicknesses. One day, in the midst of a furious storm, the order came to launch the boats, but the boats on starboard had been slammed and shattered against the hull, and those on the port side had been swept out to sea... We survived and spent several months in Hong Kong, repairing the damages. I got to know all of Africa, Asia, and Oceania, in addition to Europe, of course."

"And since the only place you had not been was America, you came here."

"That's exactly how it was, Colonel."

"I've a brother who's a sailor."

"Didn't you ever want to go to sea yourself?"

"Of course. When you're a boy you look for adventure; but then things happen. Generally, in a big family, one or two sons can choose a dangerous profession; the others have to follow their parents' wishes. Since in any case we're dealing with heroic professions, they persuade us to pick the less dangerous.

But I'm not complaining. On the contrary, I've had a successful career and will soon be made a general. My mother will be proud. She's German and as much of a foreigner as you are."

"I'm not a foreigner."

"You were naturalized?"

"No. Nationality is not conferred by a scrap of paper, however many stamps and seals it may have. I have five sons who are Chilean and... well, I don't know how to put it..."

"You're more Chilean than I am."

My father, interrupting the movement with which he was about to raise his glass to his lips, looked at the colonel: a shadow of sadness flitted over the officer's rugged features. In reply to my father's unspoken question, he answered in a voice hoarse with emotion: "I don't have any children."

***

St. Anthony's Day turned out to be memorable. Antun [Anthony] Dobronić didn't do things by halves. When we got there that June night—after walking seven blocks in the snow under the cold glitter of the stars—the house was crammed with guests drinking and engaged in lively conversation.

It was the first time that my parents had taken me to a party that was to last until dawn. I ran into several boys my own age, most of them relatives or schoolmates.

Soon I was right in the swing of things, a glass of punch in my hand. All those people turned the house into an oven, so every once in a while we stepped onto the patio or into the street to cool off and take a few puffs on some cheap cigarettes one of my cousins had brought.

In the dining room, making use of all available space, down to the last centimeter, there were two large tables covered with every conceivable comestible to be found in Punta Arenas: ham and cold cuts, chicken, an enormous stuffed turkey with a little Chilean flag on top; a salad of carrots, turnips, and potatoes; a forest of wine bottles, jugs with punch and lemonade; ten or twelve cakes that the womenfolk claimed as their specialties; and a profusion of sweets of all kinds. And—as we discovered when we sneaked outside to have a smoke— a number of champagne bottles were set out to cool, stuck in the snow of the patio.

The grown-ups, including the engaged couples, were seated at one table. The other table was for the younger generation, which included those of us from fourteen to twenty years of age. They shuffled us like cards, so each guy found himself seated next to a girl. In this lottery I wound up with a chubby, cheerful lass who, while chewing mouthful after mouthful, shrieked with laughter at every foolishness and alternately elbowed me ferociously in the ribs or equally ferociously kicked my right foot under the table. Out of sheer civility I put up with eight or ten kicks, but after the third glass of wine I began to respond by angrily pinching her thighs—a very poor idea, because she apparently liked being pinched. My oldest cousin, sitting across from me, was roaring with laughter. "What are you planning to do with so much meat, cousin?"

"He may eat as much as he can. What I have is mine to give to whom I want," the fat girl shot back.

I turned beet red and gulped down my fourth glass of wine. I felt another kick and again pinched her in reply.

The racket was so great that everyone had to yell. It seemed as if the walls were shaking. Toast followed toast. Any pretext was good enough: Toasts to "el santo,"[81] toasts to his mother and, on up the line, toasts to all Slavic ancestors, to sons, to future grandchildren, to those present, to those absent, to the deceased, and to the unborn.

The meal must have lasted no less than three hours, and woe to him who had not at least had a nibble of everything!

After the obligatory cups of strong coffee to exorcise sleepiness, we all got up. We pushed the tables against the walls, clearing the floor for dancing. Meštre Jure Pavlov, bachelor and shoemaker, took his place in a

---

[81] Commonly "name day." In this context, in Chile, "santo" refers to the person named after the saint being celebrated that day.

corner, sitting very straight on his chair, and wrested the first melody from his accordion. The opening waltz was for the host and his wife. Off they went—a stately, handsome pair—spinning around amid general applause and cheers. "Živili! Živili!"[82]

During the second half of the waltz, the guests joined in, as the house resounded with voices singing: "… tamo je selo moje, tamo je ljuibav moja."

There wasn't room for all the couples in the dining room. They spilled over to the hallways, the kitchen, and the grocery. It was my first time dancing. It was easy; besides, the fat girl was practically holding me up. My oafish cousin was dying with laughter; finally, a fifth glass of wine gave me enough courage to take away his partner, leaving him to the tender mercies of the fat girl.

We hit it off, that girl and I. She was tall and slender, with dreamy eyes and a sweet smile. Yet she could laugh merrily, and her laughter made her look beautiful. She seemed to float as she danced, especially when compared to my clumsy stomping. I felt a joy I had never before experienced and invited her outside onto the patio to look at the stars.

There were no stars. Instead, big snowflakes were falling. One settled on her nose. "I'll get rid of it for you," I said.

---

[82] "Long may they live!"

And I took advantage of the situation to steal a kiss. She fled inside. I remained on the patio, indifferent to the snow's cold caress on my forehead. After a long while I dared venture back into the house. I knew I had done something that wasn't right.

While Meštre Pavlov was taking a break, enjoying some punch, everyone else crowded around Antun, singing yet another toast just for him:

"Lijepo ime Ante,
Ante, Bog ga živio.
Koliko kapi popio,
toliko ljeta živio.
Koliko kapi toliko ljet.
Bog mu dao sretan vijek.
Koliko kapi toliko ljeta.
Sretan bio, bio, bio…
sretan živioooo!"

[Anthony is a beautiful name,
May God grant him life.
For every glass he drinks,
may he live a year,
For each glass another year.
Let God give him a happy life.
For each glass another year

Let him be happy …

let him live a happy life!]

When "el santo" had emptied his glass to the last drop, the guests surrounded his closest relative and started over:

"Ljepo ime Luka,

Luka, Bog ga živio…"

[Luka is a beautiful name,

May God grant him life…]

And after Luka they sang to Jure, Jero and Jula, Andro, Mato, Dinko and Ivo.

Since it didn't look as if the toasts would ever end, we boys set up a phonograph on the grocery counter and began to dance to a scratchy two-step record:

"I'll make a keepsake

out of the small piece of my cape

that your beautiful foot

stepped upon, stepped upon."

Unfortunately it was the fat girl's foot that kept after me. I figured the best strategy would be to invite her, too, to look at the stars. She accepted, delighted. I bowed gallantly to let her pass onto the patio, but no sooner had she stepped outside than I slammed the door shut, leaving her out in the cold and darkness, sunk up to her knees in the snow. I was sure someone would sooner or later go outside to satisfy some urgent need and would let her back in.

To my great surprise, the person who went out was my cousin.

He and the fat girl returned half an hour later without showing signs of having suffered from the cold.

The party was at its height. The men were drinking by the jugfuls, singing loudly, off key. A few couples were dancing close in the corner where Meštre Pavlov, sweating, was trying to make his accordion heard above the racket.

In the kitchen the matrons were chatting away and setting out new dishes of meat, poultry, salads, and desserts. The clock had struck three, but it would yet be many hours until daybreak, and the guests needed to refuel. Singing, dancing, and other activities were interrupted, plates were handed out, and full trays were passed around, everyone finding a spot to eat. The fat girl looked at me mockingly across her heaped plate, while elbowing a small, skinny chap who had got stuck next to her and was too timid to repulse her inroads.

"He's had it," remarked my cousin. "He won't even do as a toothpick for her."

I felt dizzy. The fat girl and the skinny guy were wobbling in front of me, and it seemed they held three or four plates that moved up and down. A picture behind them closed in on me and then retreated; faces became blurred; voices seemed very far away. I shut my eyes and kept them shut for a while, but that only made things worse; everything spun around me. I tried to stand up straight, as straight as possible. Finally I put my hand against the wall and guided myself out of the dining room. Stumbling, I reached the grocery, sat down on the floor, and leaned against a sack full of potatoes.

***

"Last night you committed the following stupidities: you smoked; you got drunk; you stepped on the toes of every girl who danced with you—you look like a bear when you dance—and if that wasn't enough, you put Tadeo 'the Pig's' daughter outside and left her in the snow."

"She wanted to go outside and… the door shut on its own."

"Don't give me that! Instead of all that shameful business you should have behaved like a gentleman and paid attention to the only girl you really liked. You probably lost her for good."

I tried to sustain my father's gaze but couldn't. For the first time I felt that he knew my feelings better than I did myself.

"Let this be a lesson to you, son. You're on the way to becoming a man. When you raise a glass, think what might be in the bottom of it, and—to be on the safe side—assume it's nothing good. At best, a brief high that can turn into sadness very shortly."

***

Winter went by and September arrived, with its yellow sun and a few flowers in the planters of the gallery. I studied hard and tried to earn better grades so as not to be scared of the final exams. It was my last year at San José. I now had two choices: I could finish high school at the Liceo Fiscal or look for a job. If I managed to get accepted at the Liceo, I could apply to the Escuela de Pilotines[83] one year later.

But some unforeseen events were about to take place.

In order to supply the regiment during maneuvers, my father had to subcontract the services of two trucks. When he went over the books, he was disappointed. It was obvious that large-scale business wasn't profitable for him. He was good at standing behind the counter, as

---

[83] At the time, one of several schools that gave instruction to students seeking to join the Marina Mercante de Chile (Chile's Merchant Marine Fleet).

a retailer, selling in small quantities at known prices. But "a promise is a promise"; so he faced his losses with fortitude.

The colonel came to thank him, and my father treated him to a few drinks and biscotti.

"You lost money, didn't you?"

"I kept my word, sir. That's all that matters."

The ensuing months were of utmost distress. I don't know whether his worries got the better of him or whether it was simply written in the stars; in any case, my father fell seriously ill. The formidable giant of a man collapsed and kept to his bed, feverish and delirious.

Everything in the house changed. Nobody seemed to be in the right place. Often I couldn't go to school because I had to help my mother. Sometimes aunts and women friends came to help out, but that wasn't the same. It was a time when all of us brothers had to grow up in a hurry. We had to keep the books, do the shopping, collect outstanding bills, deliver merchandise—in short, we had to take over every task that we had failed to notice while our father was in charge.

Dr. Béncur was no longer in Punta Arenas. Tired and ill, he had returned to his homeland "in search of repose." In his place we now had a Dr. Munizaga, an elegant man of the world who drove a luxury car. Yet he too proved to be an excellent physician. We looked up to him; he soon became our good friend, just as Dr. Béncur had been.

"What grade are you in?"

"The tenth, sir."

"Your father has a very complicated intestinal infection, apparently an old problem that's resurfacing now... maybe from his days as a sailor or his work in the gold placers. The disease is tricky, but fortunately he has a strong physique. He'll recover, but it's going to take a long time."

"How long?"

"Don't be afraid, young man. What's important is to save his life."

Dr. Munizaga came at any hour, day or night, even on Sundays. He had made it his habit to sit on the woodbox in the kitchen, and more than once, while slowly sipping a cup of coffee, he helped us with our homework. Sometimes he was a bit tipsy when he arrived and, to get over it, dozed a while, leaning his head against the wall.

Winter was well under way when my father was at last able to get up, awkwardly leaning on two canes. His pallor and extreme weight loss made him seem even taller. What a joyful day! To be sure, we weren't laughing. Quite to the contrary, our eyes filled with tears when we saw that handsome ghost walk the length and breadth of the house.

My mother fell to her knees: "Blessed Mother of God!"

As for me—relieved of the anguish that had oppressed me for so long—I wanted to sing, but held back with all my might. My father, slightly leaning forward on his canes, fixed his gaze on me—a gaze softened by pain—and asked weakly: "Što je, druže?"[84]

"Čile i Dalmacija, druže!"[85]

"Tako je, bogami!"[86]

The optimism that coursed through his veins saved his life. Thanks to his irrepressible willpower, in a couple of months he was once again the powerful man we so admired. There still were regattas to be won, boccie games to be played and, above all, many, many projects to tackle.

***

One of my father's major concerns was to find a way to buy the house in which we lived and where he had his store and, if at all possible, to acquire the empty lot on the opposite corner, so that no competitor could establish himself there. But such an undertaking required expert advice. There was only one person whom my father trusted completely. "He may be a Jew and people call him 'Penny Pincher,' but he's honest and knows his

---

[84] "What's up, pal?"
[85] "Chile and Dalmatia, pal!"
[86] "That's how it is, by God!"

business." So one Sunday morning we went to see Don Juan Radić, of whom I'd heard, but whom I had never met.

Rarely had I seen nobler and more distinguished features. His beard was clipped like Dr. Béncur's. He wore dark glasses and was sitting in a comfortable wheelchair on the spacious enclosed verandah of his house; carefully tended potted flowers perfumed the air. His wife, tall and stately, asked us to sit down and told her husband who we were.

"Oh!" exclaimed the blind man, addressing my father, "I knew at once it was you. I recognize the way you walk. So this is your oldest! He's not going to cut as imposing a figure as you do. He favors his mother. Did you know I can guess people's weight from the sound of their steps on the floor? I can hear that you are some ten kilos lighter... You've been very sick. Yes, I know all about that."

"And I want to thank you, Don Juan, for the many times you inquired about me."

"What does it cost to pick up the phone? That's my way of being in the world. Since I can't go anywhere, I call. That's how I am present at baptisms, weddings, birthdays, *santos*, and anniversaries. Darkness has improved my memory, and I forget nothing... And do you know what's best? I see everyone as they were when they were young. The women continue being beautiful;

the men, handsome, happy, contented. My world is as it was twenty years ago. None of you can make that claim. That's how God makes up for this darkness: with birdsong and the perfume of flowers."

How amazing! I expected to find an avaricious Jewish usurer and found a kindly and sentimental poet who knew my name and those of my brothers, our ages and what we were studying, and who spoke affectionately about our mother: "I have known her from the day her mother brought her outside the family house in Pučišća, virtually a newborn, so that the grannies returning from Mass could bless her... Oh! How beautiful all of that was! Happy are those who someday may see it again."

His wife brought a little tray with sweets and some port wine. Don Juan, unerringly, took the glass she handed to him: "To your healthy and that of all your family!"

"And to yours, Don Juan!"

"Jele," Don Juan said, turning to his wife, "give the boy some magazines so he can amuse himself while his father and I talk business."

I was struck by his way of speaking. In a Croatian I barely recognized—at home we used a dialect peppered with Italian and Spanish expressions—Don Juan's sentences flowed along clearly and harmoniously. For the first time I understood that in Croatian, too, there was a word for every concept. Though I held the magazine in my hands, reading it was the last thing on my mind, and I started to listen attentively. I was almost fifteen and, according to my father, would soon have to shoulder important responsibilities.

For half an hour my father explained what he wanted to do and how he planned to do it. Don Juan, pulling at his beard and twisting his mustache, listened silently. Then he summarized: "The house where you have your store is worth six thousand pesos, and the lot across the street two thousand. That's eight thousand, right? Your savings in Chilean pesos and pounds sterling amount to about four thousand. Correct?"

"Yes, that's it. I have three thousand in pesos and more or less one thousand in gold pounds."

"Fine. The pounds, being gold, are never going to depreciate. Gold derives its worth from its weight, whether or not it has the picture of St. George and the dragon on it. On the other hand, those Chilean pesos... Don Arturo Alessandri's government and his radical ministers may decide on a sudden measure that will take a ten-cent bite out of every peso. No merchant will be able to afford *llapas*.[87] Therefore, if you're going into debt, do it in Chilean pesos."

After a pause during which Don Juan seemed to be calculating in his head, he drank the remainder of his

_____

[87] Also spelled *yapas* (from *aymará*): a bonus or extra item the shopkeeper throws in with a purchase for good measure.

port and said: "This is how we'll do it: you will offer five thousand down in cash for the property in which you live and five hundred for the empty lot across the street. For the balance we'll make out some IOUs at a low interest rate, payable every six months. That way you can own everything in about two years. You will have one thousand left to supply the grocery and up the sales. You'll see, you'll be out of debt before you know it; you'll hold the title to both properties and you will still not have touched the pounds that in two years will double in value..."

"But I still have to pay you!"

"If they accept the offer I am suggesting to you and you can arrange it on your own, I won't charge you. I don't charge for advice. But if the sellers drag their feet and I have to intervene, then I will charge you, and them for being fools. In that case my fee will be ten or twelve pounds, no more."

And, laughing cordially, he added: "After all I told you, you could hardly expect me to be satisfied with a few worthless pesos."

His expression changed and, lowering his voice to a whisper, he asked: "Do you hear? The bells! It's time for High Mass. That was the first peal. Just like 'over there.' I seem to be seeing that bell tower and the pigeons flying off scared to the stone jetty of the bay of Pučišća."

It was time to leave. My father and Don Juan exchanged a warm handshake. I approached our host a bit unsure, but the blind man stretched out his hand to me and I shook it energetically. "Bravo, young fellow! You have a firm and open hand. You're generous. That means you'll never be empty-handed. Give my affectionate regards to your mother and your brothers. And if someday you feel like having a chat with an old man, do come! We blind people sometimes see more than meets the eye."

During a short period of time my father and I returned frequently to Don Juan Radić's house to settle the details regarding the two purchases. Although in the end everything worked out along the lines he suggested, Don Juan took special care to be informed about every conceivable detail of the deeds, and I had to read and reread aloud every single clause until one afternoon he told my father: "This will do. You can sign."

"What times we live in, Don Juan! Ten years ago a transaction like this would have been concluded in five minutes and with a mere handshake. Now we are beset by lawyers, notaries, and scribes, not to mention witnesses, as if we were bandits."

"That's true. Life changes as the world's population grows. I arrived in this city when it consisted of nothing more than a few houses. Nowadays there are probably fifteen thousand inhabitants. Would you dare to guess how many there'll be twenty years from now? And how many of those will be your friends or will know you well enough to put their trust in you?"

"Twenty years from now the men of today will be below ground."

"Their sons will live on; lucky those who will carry a spotless name."

After an awkward silence my father put his hand in his coat pocket and deposited twelve gold pieces on the table. "Here are the pounds I owe you, Don Juan."

With a satisfied smile, Don Juan took them and counted them, making them jingle from hand to hand. "Do you know what? I've changed my mind. Here! Take your coins and give me instead a hundred-peso bill, just don't let it be too dirty."

"But..."

"It occurs to me that with these pounds you might some day travel to Europe, you or one of your sons. That's the voyage I didn't manage to make while I still could see. And to tell the truth, what good would it do me now to travel?"

My father was overcome and barely succeeded in thanking Don Juan. who cut him short with a gesture. "We're going to celebrate this deal with a drink, and on Sunday, if the weather is nice, I'll come to 'see' your properties."

***

Dressed in a large topcoat, his hat on very straight, wearing dark glasses and leaning on a cane and on his wife's arm, Don Juan "Penny Pincher" arrived that Sunday at 3 p.m. My mother had finished her preparations in the kitchen and was on the verandah taking care of her flowers.

"Oh, woman, woman!" the blind man exclaimed from the doorstep, "always among your flowers!" and he moved slowly along the verandah naming the flowers as if he could see them.

"Carnations, hollyhocks, roses, pansies, geraniums... Oh, I see you also have basil and sage. Just like back home." And he stretched out his hands to her with the tenderness of an older brother.

He and his wife stayed the whole afternoon, praising the sweets and the hot chocolate and talking about thousands of things. Don Juan and my father at times had a separate conversation about politics. Neither of them was happy with the way things were going.

"I'm afraid," said my father, "they're just waiting for our boys to turn twenty to get us into another war."

"Or the second part of the war of 1914. Until now, despite all the years elapsed, peace has not been negotiated. Besides, the famous Armistice is nothing but a truce."

Taking advantage of a moment of silence, Doña Jele reminded her husband that it had gotten dark. He smiled: "It's always daytime for me. But you're right. Now I'll be the one to guide you."

My father offered to accompany them a few blocks. "Nowadays there are people we don't know roaming around the streets."

8

THE CHILDREN GROW UP

A violent explosion jolted me awake, and a sudden red glow lit up the bedroom as if were daytime. There was shouting, as powerful explosions followed each other in a furious crescendo. I pulled on my clothes on the run, stunned, scared stiff. My father announced succinctly: "Fire at the regimental headquarters! We might have to leave any moment. The whole house could flare up like a matchbox. Dump your stuff in the trunks... I'll go get empty sacks. I don't want to see anybody cry."

"You," he said, turning to me, "come and help me."

I ran after my father. The courtyard, covered with snow, was tinged red, and the entire sky was an immense crackling blaze as the munitions kept exploding. It was terrifying. When we returned with the sacks, relatives and friends had converged on the grocery store.

"Thank you for coming! Many thanks! But let's not lose our heads. Work in twos to fill up the sacks. If the heat gets too strong and you can smell smoke, tie up the sacks, throw them outside, and cover them with snow. I need a strong man to climb on the roof with me. We've got to carry up buckets with water to dowse the sparks that come flying over with every new blast. This won't last long. A few minutes at most. The *Santa Barbara*[88] has already blown up."

Who would climb onto the roof but Visko Damjanović, that tough, argumentative opponent of my father's!

"Like on the crossbeams of the *Saida*, right, Visko?"

"Like on the *Saida*, pal!"

All the city's inhabitants had poured out into the streets to watch the spectacle. Then sad news began to arrive: there were dead and wounded, and the fire brigade had had to withdraw, unable to accomplish anything, because there was not enough water pressure for their hoses. It didn't take long for the grocery to be converted into a field hospital. Red Cross volunteers and all the town's physicians were there. My mother and the other women were boiling water in large pots on the

---

[88] "Santa Barbara," in Chilean navy slang, referred to the powder magazine on a ship.

stove. A priest wearing his stole was sprinkling holy water.

Long minutes became one hour and yet another; but the blaze did not let up. Suddenly an incredible explosion hurled us all to the ground; windows shattered despite the wooden shutters. My father came running in: "That's it! The roof of the pavilion just collapsed! There won't be any more explosions."

He was right. All of us, taking heart, went outside to watch the conflagration die down, dissipating the infernal heat that had plagued us for almost three hours. The glaring red sky turned into gray clouds that became whiter from the water of the hoses, though they were barely able to extinguish the charred debris. Cold set in with the darkness, and men of all races and all ages crowded into our kitchen. I knew many of them, but there were at least as many whom I was seeing for the first time.

My mother and her women compatriots served coffee and brandy, and the men, once more, animatedly commented on the adventure of that terrible night. Among those present were several firefighters; they surrounded a short man of gallant bearing who held a white helmet in his hand.

"That's Don Juan Sekul, the commander of the fire brigade."

My father approached him deferentially, offering him a cup filled to the brim. "Thanks! You've had a bad night."

"Yes, no doubt, Don Juan. But yours was worse. I merely had to save my house. You had to save the city. And you did."

Don Juan Sekul smiled with a touch of sadness: "So much for us 'Austrian shitheads.' The only thing I regret is that I was hauled away from a poker game."

An officer, drenched to the skin and flushed from the cold, came to receive his orders.

The commander was precise: "The Second and the Fourth will remain on guard duty. Let the others go get some rest. But be sure they are at the barracks by 8 a.m. to take over their shift. It'll take us all day to remove and extinguish the debris."

The conflagration at regimental headquarters was unforgettable for many different reasons. During that bitter night I met many of my parents' friends whom I had never seen before. Some had come from the distant streets near the beach, from the desolate, ominous barrio Arturo Prat, the far-flung houses of Miraflores, and the Río de la Mano: "Ludi" Keko, "Banak," "Kučora" ["Ladle"], "Kenja" ["Ass"], Juan "Tiger", Juan "Pauper" "Five Mouths," "Cow's Head," and "Šporkica" ["Piglet"]. The picturesque nicknames identified them according to diverse criteria and, in general, were used like a part of their family name or even instead of it. "Black Cat" owed his nickname to the name of his store, as did "Tiger" and "Cow's Head," both butcher shop owners. "Banak" got his from his odd way of pronouncing "guanaco," and "Ludi," which means "nuts," to his outrageous shouts and wild gesticulations, which made him seem mentally unhinged. He was far from crazy, of course, and made good money delivering the most exquisite seafood delicacies—king crabs, squids, and octopuses—to the houses of the rich.

People hung around until, at nine, it became light and they took their leave one by one. My father shook hands with all of them while my mother thanked them again and again and sent greetings to each family.

Exhausted, I sat down in the chair my father always kept by the door of the grocery. What a terrible night it had been!

Just then the powerful voice of Don Visko Damjanović resounded in the kitchen, addressing my father: "I was putting things in their place out there, in the courtyard. It was a big mess." And without transition he added: "This afternoon I'm coming to have a talk with you; I don't agree with what you told me Saturday."

And he left without saying goodbye.

My father twisted his mustache and smiled, but there were tears in his eyes.

Aware of my surprise, he cleared his throat and said with a voice he tried to keep steady: "Go on, get some rest, son! Sleep all day if you want. May you never have to live through another night like this one! Go on! Get some sleep!"

It was difficult to sleep, because all day long the house was in commotion. I heard hundreds of different voices, marked by unmistakable accents: Italian, German, English, Catalan, French, and, of course, Spanish from Galicia, Asturias and Andalucía, an encouraging Babel that had found its only true language: the language of friendship, uniting everybody in these trying hours. Curiosity lured me out of bed, despite my mother's objections. It was already three in the afternoon, and it would soon be getting dark. Most visitors stayed only briefly to greet my mother and shake hands with my father. Some had something special to say or some advice to give: "Take out a good insurance, just in case. I'm not saying that this will happen a second time, but you never know..."

"If some of your merchandise was damaged and you need to replace it, come by the Society and we'll give you an advantageous loan."

"Congratulations, friend. Nobody's likely to live through such a fire twice. If this had happened to anyone else, their house would have burned down. You 'Austrians' are like rocks."

My father, serious or smiling as the comments demanded, thanked every caller and moved his *toscano* from one side of his mouth to the other.

As a result of the conflagration our whole district was left without power; my mother called me to help light the paraffin lamps that we always kept handy. (We had outages during every storm). We put two big lamps in the grocery store and two smaller ones in the kitchen. In the bedrooms we set out candlesticks, a matchbox next to each.

When I returned to the grocery, whistling lightheartedly, what I saw made me miss a note. My father stood in the middle of the store in a defensive stance, hands clenched, and framed by the doorway was the sturdy figure of Nicanor García, the Spanish milkman, my father's eternal rival in all competitions: captain of the Spanish rowing team, first-class boccie player, and undefeated weightlifter. García stood erect in his hobnailed boots, his tough-guy pants stuffed into coarse white wool stockings. his leather jacket held by a wide belt. The collar of his *huiñiporra*[89] jersey was pulled up to his ears; on his head was a bottle-green beret that had once been black. His features craggy as if hewn by a machete, his mouth pursed—the Gallego García seemed a picture of defiance. I couldn't see my father's face,

---

[89] Untwisted wool.

since he had his back turned to me, but from García's expression I guessed something very unusual was happening. My father gradually opened his fists and his body relaxed. Nicanor García took a step forward and, with an abrupt gesture, took off his beret. The flickering light of the lamp formed a sort of halo around his tousled and graying hair, softening his facial expression. Slowly he took another step and stretched out his open hand toward my father, who grasped it with the energy of a prizefighter. I couldn't tell whether they were exchanging a greeting or measuring each other's strength until the Gallego said brusquely: "You beat me here too, you blasted 'Austrian.' You have bested me with that fire! What a blaze it was... I'll shit in..."

"If you want to take a crap somewhere, don't do it here. The floor has just been washed down. And if you want your own conflagration, I'll go tonight to set fire to your dairy."

"Do you really think you could, with all the water I use in my business? Come on! If there's something that won't burn, it's my house."

"How long have we been enemies, Nicanor?"

"Always and will be until death..."

"Watch out!"

"Very well! Besides, there's this boy, your oldest, right?"

"Yes."

"Just tell him to stop bothering my little girl. Because if I catch him, I'll break him like a matchstick. Get it?"

"What I can tell you, *bogami mierda*, is that my son has good taste..."

"By which you mean..."

"That your daughter must be a lot prettier than you are!"

"Look here, you... 'Austrian' son of a...!"

"Look here yourself, you bloody fucker..."

And both of them burst out laughing. A little later they poured down several glasses of *rakija*, taking each other's measure as if this were yet another competition.

"I'm going to tell you something to make you really mad," said the milkman suddenly. "I've just bought the corner lot in the next block. I'm going to set up my oldest son there with a *boliche* and a canteen. He's got a good head for figures. What do you say to that?"

"I think that's rubbish. But I'll buy the corner opposite yours and will have any one of my boys establish a business there. That'll be an entertaining regatta."

"Are you serious?"

"No. You aren't either, are you?"

"Okay. I said it to aggravate you."

"Salud!"

"To your health!"

Nicanor García had just left, carrying as a present a *rakija* bottle my father had carefully wrapped up for him, when Visko Damjanović arrived, true to his word. My father invited him into the kitchen: "Do stay to have a bite of codfish with us. I'm going to close up early tonight. What with the darkness in the streets and the fact that nobody got any sleep last night, I don't expect customers. Even Oyarzún went home early. I can also offer you an excellent wine."

"Great! A good dish of cod and a glass of good wine never get turned down."

Before the two friends settled down to eat, they became absorbed in one of their long conversations. They were worried about the general unrest. Rumors had it that the Chilean government might fall at any moment and that the army would take over. So much for Chile. But in Europe, too, there were odd goings-on. In Italy the puny king had handed the government over to a strange individual without a drop of blue blood who paraded around insolently, dressed in a black shirt with a tricolor sash draped across his belly. The Austrian Empire had become a pathetic little debt-ridden republic full of war widows. Bad stuff!

It wasn't a conversation to hold my interest. I was much more concerned about not having gone to see Isabelita Arancibia.

Whenever we ate in the kitchen, which we did every day in winter, Sundays included, we all had assigned places at the table. My father sat at the head, the three older brothers to his left on a long bench placed against the wall; the two younger boys were at the other end. My mother kept the entire right side for herself so she could move the soup tureens, dishes, and pots and pans, and serve. That's the way things were done in her house from the time of her grandparents on, and the old custom was never changed unless there was a guest, who would be invited to sit to the right of the master of the house.

So Don Visko occupied the visitor's spot and, gallantly raising his glass with studied courtesy, he toasted: "To your health, señora!"

My mother smiled and moistened her lips in the wine. Then she fetched the steaming serving dish of cod stewed with potatoes, tomatoes, raisins, and spices. What an exquisite fragrance pervaded the house! Mama heaped the food on our plates. A long silence ensued during which we did nothing except eat, taking care not to slurp the gravy, make any other inappropriate noise, or blow on the food.

"Your sons are gentlemen, ma'am. Congratulations!"

My mother invited Don Visko to have a second helping, which he accepted with pleasure, raising his eyes heavenward.

"It's not every day..."

His glance fixed itself on the wall just above my head, and his expression tensed. He stretched out his long arm and pointed with his index finger, aiming as with the tip of a lance: "But, but..." he spluttered, turning furiously toward my father: "You have that SOB up there!"

Then, restraining himself with a huge effort, he addressed my mother: "Señora, I respect your honorable house with all my soul; but you will have to forgive me. I can't go on eating with this bloody tyrant facing me."

My father burst out laughing: "Don't be melodramatic, Visko. If you don't want to look at Francis Joseph, you have Karageorge[90] on the other side or Don Arturo[91] in the middle."

"Francis Joseph no longer exists!"

"But exist he did! Or are you going to deny that? Don't talk nonsense, Damjanović. Francis Joseph at least had stamina. Let's see how long that Serb will last. And please, let's not keep harping on the same topic. This codfish deserves to be enjoyed in peace."

---

[90] Serbian leader (1766 or 1768–1817) in the first revolution against the Turks (1804–1813) and founder of the Karadjordević Dynasty. King Alexander I of Yugoslavia was his descendant. *Kara* means "black" in Turkish.
[91] Chilean president Arturo Alessandri Palma.

But seeing that his obstinate friend remained out of sorts, my father commanded: "Take down all three pictures."

"Why all three?"

"Because if I told you what I think of them, Visko, you wouldn't want to look at any one of them."

"You're not going to remove the president of Chile!"

"And why ever not? Isn't he an Italian with a nose as red as that of the tailor Barassi?"

"I think that's a lack of respect."

"Ha! Just watch how much they respect him when five years are up, even though he might have done a good job."

"This is a republic!"

"And how would a republic fare in Yugoslavia?"

"That can't happen. We have a king of our own..."

"And if he turns out to be bad king? Then what?"

"You're impossible. You don't want to see reason. Why should he be a bad king?"

"And why should he be good? Do you want us to keep asking the same question five thousand times?"

"We have the support of the Allies, and France is charged with organizing the economy of the new nation.

Did you know that the legend on the *dinar*[92] is in Croatian, Serbian, and French?"

"Bravo! I just hope French is easier than German; but I pity the kids who have to learn yet another foreign language to find out how much they have to pay for bread. I can't see much difference between one foreign domination and another. At least I was used to the old one. I'll try to get used to the new. Tomorrow I'll look for a portrait of the French president."

The discussion threatened to turn ugly, but perhaps the fatigue from the preceding night, or the cold seeping in through the cracks of doors and windows, and almost certainly the respect Damjanović felt for the "honorable house" calmed the tempers, and Don Visko took his leave with elaborate expressions of praise for the excellent meal. When the door was opened, letting in a sudden blast of penetrating cold, Don Visko exclaimed: "It's like stepping onto the deck of the *Saida* in the North Sea."

"That's right, pal," my father cheerfully yelled back.

The swirling wind and snow appeared to be lifting up Damjanović's tall, powerful figure, wrapped in the loose folds of his wide overcoat.

***

---

[92]Yugoslav monetary unit.

Although kinships and friendships remained unalterable—the same conversations, the same visits, the same pastimes, the same vices, and the same interests—something was definitely changing; every day something vanished, gradually, almost imperceptibly. But after several weeks or several months, these changes suddenly became evident, as if they had occurred abruptly. I'm not sure what disappeared first, the canes or the bowler hats, the gaiters or the stiffly starched collars, but suddenly all those items were seen no longer.

Then—or was it earlier?—the few carefully trimmed beards disappeared, and at last there was a noticeable struggle to diminish the notorious size of the mustaches.

The mustaches! Ah, the mustaches! Nothing that had been cast aside had managed to defend itself with as much determination as the mustache. Despite the trend to suppress it altogether, without a trace, the mustache fought resolutely to survive, even if reduced to its minimal manifestation. Nobody, not even the most fanatic partisan of clean-shaven faces, dared to get rid of his mustache with one heroic sweep of the razor. Instead, mustaches at first had their tips trimmed, then lingered on as rectangular mini-brushes, covering the entire upper lip; still later, as a pair of Chaplinesque flies; and finally, as... nothing.

Whenever a kum or a barba turned up with some innovation under his nose, my father roared with laughter and twisted the ends of his majestic, ineradicable mustache, which, while the other men's kept getting smaller, reached Cyclopean dimensions.

"For two years now I've been watching how they have been eliminating the mustache, hair by hair, until they've made it disappear. If that's what they wanted, why didn't they shave it off in one go, instead of playing the fool all this time?"

"We haven't been playing the fool; we have simply followed the fashion," Kum Grgo objected. "The same thing happened in Europe. Now even the kings are clean-shaven."

"So mustaches too have something to do with politics?"

"No doubt. I think a loyal Yugoslav ought to shave, since that's what the king does."

"Fine. So what would you think if I turned Orthodox, since that's the king's religion?"

"You don't have to go quite that far," Kum Grgo said defensively.

"I couldn't agree more," concurred my father, twisting his mustache with both hands. However absurd it might seem, the mustache became something of a symbol for ideological conservatism, as well as for militarism and intransigence. But on the other hand, mustachelessness represented the intransigence of the majority, dazzled by a modernism that not everybody could grasp to the fullest.

To be sure, between the two extremes there was no middle ground, neither in the present nor in the foreseeable future. Things were headed for a clash between a clear anti-mustache majority and a hardheaded, obstinate mustachioed minority.

One thing was certain, though: the proprietors of the hairless upper lip had forever lost the capability to hide a mocking smile under a bushy mustache.

But in politics there are no definitive defeats, and what is repudiated one day can be rehabilitated at any moment; everything depends on the circumstances. The brand-new Yugoslav Club had been converted into the arena of constant guerrilla warfare in which two equally stubborn and powerful forces confronted each other: those who had adapted to the new order in Yugoslavia, and the young people who tried to adapt the new order to their more progressive and daring ideas. The new caste that was beginning to form, made up of toadies, go-getters, nouveaux-riches, and some merchants willing to make profits with or without the king's blessing, seemed to have as its banner a face as hairless as a watermelon peel. And then, naturally, the young men, just to be obnoxious, began to keep their mustaches.

Two camps that until that moment had been tacitly acknowledged now openly declared themselves. From then on any debate was decided beforehand, and one could foresee its result simply by taking a census of mustaches versus solitary noses.

As was to be expected, in the midst of this controversy there surfaced an element that was to some extent conciliatory because of its very ambiguity: a small, elongated mustachelet, traced with a razor—a miniature replica of the arrogant mustache of times past. It was a way out for the easygoing, the impartial, and the timorous. And it was likewise the needle of the scale in the vague and subtle internal struggle. Ever since the appearance of the new mustachelet, no one could predict a majority or rely, ahead of time, on the clear result of a vote. A board of directors might have to resign, censured in the most opprobrious terms, yet when the moment came to elect new officers, the very same committee might be re-elected. Nobody could explain how, but that's the way it was. And nothing was gained by counting mustaches, because those parodies of mustaches had lost all significance. Except, perhaps, to proclaim boldly the inexhaustible sense of Slavic humor.

In agitated meetings where the hotheads climbed on the billiard tables while the calmest took their seats with their backs to the wall, both hands firmly grasping their canes, the cauldron boiled, threatening to explode any minute; but no blood was ever shed.

And about two or three in the morning, after byzantine discussions whose beginnings and endings seemed inextricably entangled, the tempers, however high they might have been, cooled down, and people came to their senses as the icy outside air hit their faces, freezing their breath. This was especially true if the next day was Sunday and there was something important to do.

***

Mustachioed, semi-mustachioed, and clean-shaven men started invading the grandstands of the soccer stadium at an early hour, trying by sheer force to prevent any non-Yugoslav from garnering a seat; at the other end of the stadium a vociferous crowd of Spaniards monopolized all the seats for their people. It was a Sunday of bellicose euphoria: "Sokol" versus "Español," the two colossi of the local "kicking" scene.

Both *barras*,[93] rivals from time immemorial in all athletic competitions, were on hand, fierce, arrogant, aggressive, and uncompromising like fighting cocks, ready to come to blows. The rest of the public was happy: whatever the outcome, the afternoon promised to be most entertaining.

---

[93] Groups of fans.

Both teams ran out onto the field as an annoying breeze sprang up, carrying off the "hurrahs" of the fans and blowing the first grains of dirt into the eyes of the spectators.

The red T-shirts of the Spaniards undoubtedly evoked *tardes de toros*.[94] "*Olé muchachos!* Let them have it! Let's draw blood! *Olé!* Kill those 'Austrians'!" Offended, their blood boiling, the Yugoslavs yelled their aggressive ditty so it could be heard above the wind:

"Stupaj naprijed Sokole, Sokole, Sokole
na španjolske lopove, lopove, lopove..."

[Onward, Falcons, Falcons, Falcons,
against the Spaniards bandits, bandits, bandits...]

The wind favored the "Español." Without major effort they scored two goals in a few minutes. The "Sons of the Fatherland"[95] produced banners, castanets, and bagpipes and danced so the stands seemed about to collapse; the poor "Austrians" chewed on their mustaches or the place where their mustaches used to be.

Another Spanish goal. That made three. The Hispanic fans intensified their jig, accompanied by deafening beating on the metal signs that proclaimed the

---

[94] Literally, afternoon festivities at the bullfight arena.
[95] Term "criollos" sometimes use to refer to Spaniards.

virtues of Sloan's Liniment and Queen Victoria cigarettes. The Slavs seemed ready for collective suicide.

That's how things were at halftime as both teams went to recess. The Spanish fans invaded their dugout: everybody wanted to see and embrace the heroes.

There was music and exuberance. The Yugoslav fans stayed put, elbows on their knees, their faces between their hands. Unnoticed, the half-bent, slight figure of Don Pablo Drpić got up from one of the lower rows. He was the only one to go to the dugout, and from the door he glanced at the disheartened players: "Cheer up, guys! The wind scored those three goals. Now it's our turn. And you know what? Use the advantage as soon as you can. The wind might shift suddenly."

The captain of the team—tall, solid, and young— drew himself up to his full height: "And where are the others... those who are good at singing, those who holler?"

"They didn't want to get you down with their dejection. Cheer up, boys! Our turn has come! The wind is impartial... There's the whistle! Go on! Mark my words: everything will change!"

On the wings of the hurricane, which whistled with unrelenting fury, the "Sokols" scored the three goals in three minutes. Then, suddenly, total calm ensued. Now tied, the teams fought over the ball, using spirited brute force rather than skill, while in the stands Slavs and

Spaniards jumped up and down, shouting themselves hoarse: Meštre Pavlov's accordion and the Gallego Barrepi's bagpipes insulted each other in discordant riffs in the midst of a huge uproar full of obscenities and violent gestures. But despite the shoving and the show of force, no more goals were scored and the match finished in a tie.

By that time the sun was sinking slowly among red clouds behind the western hills. As they left the field, the members of the two opposing teams exchanged handshakes, and their fans formed a caravan along the streets on their way to the square, playing their guitars, castanets, tambourines, and bagpipes, their accordions, tamburitzas,[96] mandolins, and harmonicas.

But during the goodbyes someone blurted out a warning: "Next time blood will flow!"

***

The old small-town customs persisted even when, little by little, they adapted themselves to the new trends. Thus, for example, there was the traditional Sunday promenade around the square in the mornings, while the band, confined in the kiosk, made the windowpanes rattle as it played a vibrant Prussian march; but in the afternoons the same promenade was extended toward the sea along the elegant Roca Street. And that's how it

---

[96] Stringed instruments of varying size used in Croatia, related to the Bulgarian tamboura.

was for years, until a group of youths changed the route by ninety degrees and started to walk back and forth along the sunny sidewalks of Bories Street. And this new custom prevailed and may well last into the distant future.

Changing the itinerary did not, however, change either the intention or the significance of the promenade. The promenaders were (and will continue to be) boys and girls who had come to consider themselves young adults, and the soon-to-be mothers-in-law who popped up as if by chance weighing the qualities of their potential sons-in-law. Slanders, calumnies, and predictions were fabricated; illnesses, bad business deals, the next wedding, and the likelihood or improbability of a hard freeze that night were discussed.

The Sunday promenade allowed the two factions to exhibit—with a touch of arrogance and boastfulness—the latest dictates of fashion. The young women shortened their skirts at the rate of several centimeters per week, converted their hats into bonnets, started wearing flesh-colored stockings and absurdly high heels, painted violet or gray circles under their eyes, and traced heart-shaped mouths with purple lipstick.

The young men, not to lag behind, widened, narrowed, and once more widened the hems of their trousers; returned to short, straight jackets with three buttons, then reduced the buttons to one; wore double-breasted waistcoats again; sported hats of different colors, wide-brimmed, narrow-brimmed, with bands of varying width; for a while everybody fancied coats down to their heels; next, coats were shortened and then lengthened again... And so it went, one innovation following the next, each one fading more quickly than the preceding one.

All this while people married, died, traveled, or simply lived. Between May and September I attended eight weddings of relatives and friends. All these weddings seemed regrettably the same: the same cramped houses invaded by detachments of guests, numerous enough to fill ten such abodes; the same impertinent kids darting in and out between the legs of the adults; the same reprimanding mothers; the same overcoats heaped on the bed of the master bedroom; and the same presents, the same drinks, the same cakes. It even seemed that the groom and the bride were always the same.

I also had to accompany my father to several funerals. I even had to help carry a coffin. That was at the funeral of a poor Dalmatian who—ailing and sick—used to sell fish from door to door. He died alone and abandoned in his miserable room; a group of neighbors bought a modest black box, but there were only six of us to shoulder the coffin, lower it into the grave, and throw in the first few handfuls of earth.

"That's life! It treats some well and others badly; but not even the wealthiest man in the world knows how he will end up. Keep that fact very much in mind!" I thought my father was about to launch into one of his long pronouncements, but actually we walked many blocks in complete silence. Only when we reached the top of our street and the facade of the regimental headquarters was outlined against the red evening sky did my father add, as if to himself: "God does not give us all we ask, but He does give us more than we deserve."

***

The National Day of Yugoslavia rolled around, and the paper *El Magallanes* published on its front page a large photo of King Alexander and another of the consul in Punta Arenas, Don Vicente Kusanović, with lengthy and appropriate greetings to the local Yugoslav community.

"Just let Visko Damjanović come by now. I have a few comments to make to him."

But Visko Damjanović had decided not to listen to those comments and didn't show up. In view of that, my father determined that I was the one who needed to hear what he had to say. He picked up the paper and asked me if I had carefully read everything pertaining to Yugoslavia, its king, and its consul. When I replied in the affirmative, he cleared his throat, exhaled a mouthful of smoke from his tenth *toscano* of the day, and said: "Look at this oddity: Whom do you suppose the king has chosen to represent him? One of those know-it-alls who hold eloquent speeches at every meeting and who belong to the Club Hípico,[97] the Red Cross, the Fire Brigade, or the Boy Scouts? Or one of those businessmen importing sardines and olives, who sell us sauerkraut at ten times its value? Well, no. He picked a working man of humble origin who can barely read but who is honest and decent. Up to now his only accomplishment is to have been the first to harvest carrots in Magallanes, to have raised pigs on turnips and to have produced cabbages weighing five kilos each. That's Consul Kusanović for you! And let the others chew on their mustaches or the empty space they have below their noses."

Give or take a bit, that was the unvarnished truth. In the fierce struggle for the consulship, all the stops had been pulled out, and many names of real or fictitious merit had been tossed around. Half a dozen tailcoats ended up stored with mothballs in their pockets, joined by a number of shirtfronts shining like porcelain and as many top hats of English provenance. Finally emerging from this consular fray was a former shepherd from Pražnice (near the stone quarries in the interior of the island of Brač), a self-taught grower of turnips and

---

[97] Club for owners of race horses.

carrots, a pig breeder and wholesale butcher, owner of an establishment located half a block from the square.

But from the very day he was appointed, Don Vicente became the target of attacks; some, half-justified, dwelt on his lack of education; the rest insidiously ridiculed him in a thousand ways, even mocking his overly deferential turns of speech and social mannerisms.

If the far-off king learned of these petty local intrigues, he gave absolutely no sign of it and let matters take their course—a permanent affront to some and a cause for rejoicing for the majority, whose origins, when it came right down to it, were as humble as or even humbler than those of the Honorable Señor Consul. It could be said that most people favored him, if for no other reason than class solidarity, whereas the elite of nouveaux-riches and frustrated intellectuals kept mulling over the bitter defeat.

***

A new force began to make itself felt in the Yugoslav community: the sons of immigrants, the criollos, now were getting to be of age and had to be allowed to express themselves in Spanish at meetings held in the Yugoslav Club.

"This is the first symptom of a long battle we are bound to lose. The young will sweep us forward unless we learn to march at their speed."

"That's not surprisinig, Visko," said my father, blowing the ashes off his cigar. "We'll have problems with our children, but they will have problems with theirs. That's the way the world turns."

"No one knows, indeed."

Outside the wind started to blow.

The children were truly beginning to cause problems. Every day one could hear something odd, out of place, in the uncomplicated order of the lives of these simple people, attached to their old norms and customs. Rumors had it that a certain girl or a certain boy had gotten mixed up with the wrong crowd; that two beardless youths had knifed each other over the favors of a more mature than merry widow; that the fiancé of so-and-so had disappeared prior to the wedding but was expected for the baptism; that…

The dramatic and the picturesque went hand in hand, as in the case of Popić, the old shoemaker, whose little shop was on one of the back streets of the "Austrian Quarter," renamed "Yugoslav Quarter" for its inhabitants. Marko Popić had been sitting at his workbench every day for more than twenty-five years, putting on soles and repairing the most decrepit workman's boots, as well as the most delicate feminine footwear. Almost ten years ago he had sent his only son, who had arrived with him from Europe, to school in Santiago. The boy wanted to be a physician, and Marko Popić was determined that his son should be one, no matter what the cost.

His son's absence, the silence at home, the monotony at work, and the cold, lonely nights led Marko, widowed almost from the time of his arrival in Punta Arenas, to take a wife. He married "la Tránsito," a dark and robust Chilota who did his laundry and prepared his meals. Father Savarino blessed the marriage in the sacristy of the Don Bosco Church, and the bridal couple and their witnesses celebrated the event with a bottle of port.

At the news that the son had been awarded his degree and would be coming home to visit his father, Marko Popić imagined that the best present for him would be a handsome bronze plaque saying in big letters, "Dr. Luka Popić." He went to see his good friend, the blacksmith Erwin Müller, a German with formidable fists, a huge blond mustache, and a thunderous voice, the only one capable of forging the plaque Marko envisioned.

After several attempts, representing weeks of labor, Marko could finally put his hands on a huge, heavy plaque with letters in relief, legible from a distance of half a block.

The smith, sweaty, wearing a canvas apron pockmarked by molten metal, smiled a satisfied smile as he painstakingly went over the outline of each letter with a file. A generous glass of brandy marked the completion of the project. Popić paid the modest sum Müller asked for and went home with the plaque wrapped in newspaper.

The son arrived. Serious, elegant, distant, almost a stranger, he felt ill at ease on the crude chairs in his father's house and looked down on the poor Chilota, who smiled at him with maternal affection. Marko seemed to understand: "You'll be staying just a few days, right?"

"Very few; I'll have to return by the same boat that brought me."

"You'll probably want to see your old friends... the city has changed so much... Well, what do I know? Go, son, and come tomorrow to have a meal of codfish with us."

La Tránsito went all out preparing the meal and even asked a neighbor, a compatriot of her husband's, to help her. Marko bought two bottles of the finest wine and put on the tie that he hadn't worn since his wedding day.

It got dark and the clock struck seven. Then eight. Then nine. On the stove the overcooked cod turned cold. The plates, the silverware, and the two bottles were waiting on the table.

Marko Popić understood. He sat down to eat in silence. La Tránsito sobbed in a corner. Marko gulped down both bottles, almost without taking a breath. The volcano he was carrying inside erupted. Blaspheming, grunting with fury, he went to his shop, unwrapped the bronze plaque, took his shoemaker's hammer and four large nails and, before the eyes of the astonished Chilota, who had followed him and was greatly upset, threw the front door wide open, dumped the plaque on the ground, and nailed it to the doorstep. The moon made the relief stand out, and the inscription "Dr. Luka Popić" shone in the night. Then, having recovered his serenity, Marko turned to his wife: "Here's the doormat you have asked me for so many times."

And he banged the door shut.

***

At that time I received a notification I had almost ceased to expect. The maritime company where I had applied for a job offered me a position as purser in a ship that was to arrive in four days.

Those four days changed my whole life. I left the Liceo, barely saying good-bye to my fellow students. I walked all over the barrio to visit the people with whom I had lived all my life. It was not without a feeling of pain that I went along the streets where I had played as a child and, more recently, had hung out as a youth.

My mother, without my realizing it, had gone to the stores she usually patronized and had bought me everything I would need, from socks to half a dozen black ties, "the type officers on ships use." Poor Mama! She would say these words so proudly, though she was hurting inside, hiding her pain behind a smile and a calm gaze. And how she would pray at night!

My father accompanied me to the gangplank. He shook my hand firmly, then immediately turned around and started to walk off very straight, his powerful steps echoing along the pier, deserted at this early hour. Without a backward glance, he strode up the street.

I picked up my suitcase and my canvas bag, slowly climbed onboard, and looked for the purser. He personally showed me to my bunk in a cabin I was to share with another bookkeeper, had me get into my uniform and set me to work copying payroll tables.

When the boat set sail two days later, I briefly went on deck to reply to the salutes of my brothers and my father bidding me farewell from the pier.

9

FOREVER

Nine long years went by in a flash. I went from port to port and ship to ship, along the coasts of South and North America. I already had earned three thin gold stripes on a white background—the accountant's stripes—when the Second World War broke out. At first no one was particularly concerned, but after a few months navigation became dangerous, and neutral ships, painted gray, were marked by huge flags on both sides of their hull for identification. We navigated in the dark, our portholes covered by wooden shutters; on deck you could see life boats and anti-aircraft guns.

During those nine years I returned home many times to spend a few days with my family. My father showed me—with legitimate pride—how the grocery store had expanded and spoke with enthusiasm about his current great projects: a house for each of his sons (two of my brothers were already married) and the founding of a company with these sons to do business on a large scale.

But when war was declared, all his enthusiasm, optimism, and joie de vivre crumbled all at once. As I was getting ready to leave on that occasion, he put his hand on my shoulder as he had done when I was a boy, gazed at me profoundly, and, biting his already grizzled mustache, told me with a tired, slow, and sad voice: "That's what it's coming to. It's the end. All we've accomplished in this devilishly hard life won't be worth a thing. This time the world is going down the drain for good. There's so much hate, so much insanity; there is no Faith... It'll be a cruel war. No one will be able to escape."

I left, profoundly disturbed. My father had ceased to be the strong man, immutable as a rock and unbending as an oak. For some reason I remembered an incident that had nothing to do with the gravity of the moment: a group of my father's compatriots once came to offer him the honor of being one of the men to carry the platform with the statue of the recently canonized St. John Bosco in a procession. My father looked at them indulgently, smiled vaguely, and excused himself: "My bones have been aching lately. It's the old rheumatism, you know..."

When the delegation had left, slightly disappointed, he burst out laughing and declared: "The day hasn't dawned when I'd carry an Italian on my shoulders, however saintly he might be!"

That's what he was like: true to himself, above all. This meant, according to his own words, that his friends were real friends and his enemies (he didn't feel like anyone's enemy) also were real enemies.

***

It was a bad voyage. Off Coquimbo we ran into a terrifying storm. The cargo shifted; our ship listed perilously. We had a rough time saving the boat and setting everything to rights again. Besides that, we received warnings not to sail at night, to anchor with our lights out, all of which stressed out the crew. We felt short-tempered and lived virtually locked up in our cabins, drinking more than was good for us and sleeping in snatches, in a never-ending state of anxiety. I heaved a sigh of relief when we tied up at the pier of Punta Arenas one evening.

It was drizzling and cold. I threw my black raincoat over my uniform and pulled my hat down to my eyes. I got home around nine. There still was light in the grocery, and the little bell tinkled cheerfully when I opened the door. I was going to holler a greeting when my younger brother appeared on the threshold of the back door, signaling me to keep silent.

"What's going on?" I asked anxiously.

"Papa is very sick."

Mama was in the kitchen next to the warm stove, a rosary in her hands; my brothers, around the table, were finishing supper. Don Pedro, the baker, white-haired, old, and with a slight tremor to his chin, was sitting in a corner and was the only one to smile when he shook hands with me.

"We're waiting for the doctor," said my mother.

And no one said another word.

I took off my raincoat and felt irked by the reflection of my golden stripes. I lit a cigarette and went up to Alexander: "What's the matter with him?"

Alexander shrugged his shoulders and shook his head: "No one can figure it out. Perhaps he simply feels like dying."

Don Pedro came up to me: "The time has come for us old folks to depart. So many have gone on already! Yesterday one, today another, tomorrow yet another... We have to make way for the young generation; that's only fair..."

He paused and then added: "Now that all of you are here, I'm no longer needed. I'm leaving. I'll come by tomorrow. Good night."

The little bell above the door tinkled as Don Pedro left, and almost immediately it tinkled again. Oyarzún, hunched, his hair and mustache ashen, entered, dragging his feet, followed by the stout Rosalía. God almighty! How long had I known that man? I seemed to have memories of him antedating those involving my father.

Oyarzún came up to me respectfully and proffered his rough, stiff hand, which I shook warmly. A dim memory—a cart, a storm, children crying—brought tears to my eyes.

Rosalía busied herself with clearing the table, throwing more coal into the stove, and boiling water to brew coffee. Zvonko and Alexander went to fasten the shutters and close up the grocery. We heard the curfew being sounded at the regimental base. There we were— five brothers exchanging glances and looking at our mother in silence, hoping that the inevitable would not occur, though we sensed it next to us, in our midst.

The doctor arrived: dark-skinned, swarthy, agile, rather short, smiling and dynamic. Followed by my mother and Alexander, he went into the bedroom where my father was lying in his wide bed.

Shortly afterward my mother, leaning on Alexander's shoulder, left the bedroom, unable to refrain from sobbing. The doctor made a sign for me to enter.

In the filtered light of the night lamp, I saw the sharp profile of an old man whom I could barely recognize. Emaciated, with sunken cheeks, eyes shining feverishly, hair white as snow clinging to his forehead, his mustache unkempt, he was nothing but a vague shadow, remote, ridiculous, like a caricature of that powerful man who, erect at the stern of a boat commanded his crew in a firm voice: "*Jedan, dva.*"

Lost in a vague drowsiness, my father was unaware of my presence, and I looked at him for a long while, not wanting to convince myself of the inevitable truth. He would never again ask me: "*Što je, druže?*"

Overcome by fatigue from many sleepless nights, my mother and my brothers went to rest. Fat Rosalía slumbered, leaning on the table, and Oyarzún took a nap next to some sacks of corn in the store.

The young doctor, Chilean to the marrow, sat on the woodbox. He was the third physician to sit there, from the far-off days of Dr. Béncur and, more recently, Dr. Munizaga... I served him a cup of coffee, and, having taken a sip, he began to talk: "Your father's case is an odd one. He isn't old enough to be dying of old age; and he doesn't have a definite illness, or, at least, not a fatal one."

"Nonetheless..."

"Yes. He is dying. I think he won't live past tomorrow. His heart is already too weak."

A prolonged silence descended over the entire house, except for the distant barking of dogs and the monotonous tick-tock of the clock on the dining room wall. Through the half-open door we could see the faint glow of the bedside lamp shining on the dying man.

"So that's what he lived and fought for during more than forty years in this wretched land!"

"Don't say that." The doctor gently cut me short. "You were born here, have lived here, and have tried to leave this place; therefore you think that your father—and so many like him—has sacrificed himself for nothing, that his life was meaningless, that he accomplished nothing. How wrong you are, my friend!"

And when I looked at him questioningly, in silence, he continued: "Ever since I got to Punta Arenas, right after finishing my studies, some three years back, I have not ceased to marvel at this reality—so beautiful and so impossible. Everywhere there is evidence of the presence of Man, of his struggle, his effort and his triumph... To create a city like this is midway between the absurd and the heroic. At first glance it seems to make no sense that anyone would have wanted to live in this strange climate, one of the harshest in the world, and, no doubt, the most inhospitable. Only indomitable people, courageous and energetic, with iron constitutions, could have done this. But what was it that propelled them to do all they did?... Do you have an answer for this question?"

"I never put this question to myself."

"Just consider. They arrived, at least the first ones did, lured by the chimera of gold, dazzled by the vague rumors, heard in their childhood, of fabulous wealth in America. And suddenly they were most cruelly disabused. It was not a question of picking up gold on the riverbanks or the edge of forests; rather—as in the tales of dragons and giants—they had to pass through gates that were under an evil spell, cross moats where venomous snakes writhed, get round impassable abysses—face as many difficulties and sacrifices you can conceive of. But what motivated them? Their family, poor and distant, that had stayed behind gazing at the horizon from a stony island in the Adriatic? Their sweetheart? Their young wife gestating a new life? Here's the answer to the question you never put to yourself. Why all of this, why the effort, why the sacrifice? For something as natural and eternal as life itself—simply for love's sake."

A cock crowed in the distance, barely audible, then another one closer by, and yet another. The tick-tock of the clock marked the cold nocturnal silence like a strange hour-grinding machine. Time went by slowly, slowly… "Another cup of coffee?"

"Yes, please."

He drank his coffee, savoring it; he left the cup on the edge of the table, once more took his seat on the woodbox, and lit a cigarette: "I was told that barely ten years ago this city was only half of what it is at present. You yourself, coming and going as you do, must have noticed. Now Punta Arenas is a modern city, with those old pompous buildings of European architecture, as well as new graceful constructions; commerce is booming; there are good theaters, splendid schools, all kind of industries and activities... And you, who as you told me have seen your father put down the stones for the sidewalks, one by one—aren't you proud of that? It's easy enough for a big entrepreneur to say 'I'm going to do this or that; the difficult part is to find someone to actually bring the idea to fruition, materially and physically. That's where the Yugoslavs came in—the shitty 'Austrians'—to do everything that needed to be done. And they did."

Surprised, I looked at the young doctor who spoke to me with such enthusiasm about my land and my people, and I felt ashamed not to have known how to perceive all that, of not having understood the essence of the life that had ebbed and flowed around me from the outset.

"But they did more. Much more. And they keep on doing it. My profession takes me everywhere... that's why I know; because I have seen it, because I am seeing it every day."

He inhaled his cigarette and savored the smoke, letting it escape slowly from between his teeth. His voice seemed somewhat distant: sleep was getting the better of me; but hear him I did.

"Some behind the counter, like your father; others, in a butcher's apron splattered with blood; still others risking their lives gathering their nets in the midst of a storm. I admire the greengrocer and the fishmonger with their full baskets crying their wares in broken Spanish. And then there are the carpenter, the mechanic, the humble tinsmith; the peon on an estancia, the shearer; the man who loses his lungs in the freezing cold of the meatpacking plants or next to the furnaces of the factories…"

The doctor moved around the stove and brought me a cup of coffee. "Don't you fall asleep on me, sailor."

He went back to the woodbox, sipping his steaming coffee, and continued: "And of course then there are the rich cattlemen who drive around in their cars and marry their daughters off to army or navy officers. And the wealthy merchants… no doubt more than one thief among them. A few years hence, you'll see how the sons of the greengrocer, the baker or the fisherman, and also those of some *estanciero* will become lawyers, engineers, professors. Already there are two physicians practicing here whose fathers are *bolicheros*. That generation, our generation, the one you and I belong to, is on the march. And that will be the generation in charge of ruling this country in a few years' time, and that's when you will see Yugoslav surnames in many high places, in important positions, carrying the greatest responsibility."

"And do you know why? Because the Yugoslav became integrated into the Chilean culture. You are criollo; but there are many who are mestizos, half their blood Chilean. And the moment will come when there'll be many blondes with a Chilote surname and dark-skinned chaps like me with a Yugoslav name. They already exist, but they are still children and don't know what sort of parents they have or what sort of grandparents they had."

***

Dawn came with a white, diffused light. Again the cocks crowed and the dogs barked. From the grocery store Oyarzún emerged like a shadow and went to wake up Rosalía, who was snoring, hunched over the table exactly as she had been for many hours.

Pale, our chins covered with stubble and our eyes irritated from smoke and lack of sleep, the doctor and I went to the bathroom to freshen up a bit. We then entered my father's bedroom and I opened the curtains to let in the morning light. I couldn't hear him, but I saw that his lips formed the question: "*Što je, druže?*"

Barely lifting a white and bony hand, he motioned me to sit on the edge of his bed: "Father Juan will soon come to give me my passport... Be sure he is served a good cup of coffee."

He coughed and the effort caused the veins in his neck to swell: "That's from the *toscano*s."

After a long pause that prompted the doctor to take his pulse, he said slowly, barely articulating each of the words: "I am leaving, son. You are the eldest... Take care of your mother and... stay here, with your brothers... in what is ours... what is yours."

He cleared his throat weakly and said in a slightly clearer voice: "I'm thirsty. Give me some water."

Helping him to sit up, I shuddered when I became aware of the lightness of that once so powerful body; controlling my trembling, I offered him a sip of water.

"Thank you, son," he murmured, smiling faintly. His wide-open eyes shone, and he said in a firm voice: "Give me your hand, *compañero*!"[98]

And with his last energy, for the briefest instant, he shook my hand as strongly as in his good times. Soon he dropped his head and expired.

Father Juan entered almost at a run and started to administer the Extreme Unction. I went up to the window and rested my forehead on the pane so they wouldn't see me cry.

***

---

[98] Close friend, partner, pal.

When we returned from the funeral, the house still smelled of flowers and incense, although almost all the windows were open.

My mother, surrounded by a group of fellow countrywomen in mourning, finished saying the rosary, and then, at the urging of her neighbors, agreed to lie down for a bit. Rising from her chair, she looked around slowly and murmured: "He isn't here. He isn't anywhere. Never again will we hear his steps, his laughter, his shouts, his songs. He is no longer with us. This house is empty now. He isn't here…"

We looked at her, not knowing what to do or say.

Behind me was heard, drowning in sobs, the hoarse voice of the Chilote Oyarzún: "No, ma'am. He has not left. He's here… Look at him in his five sons. He will never leave… He has stayed here, forever.